FOLLOWING THE DREAM

FOLLOWING THE DREAM

George Dalton

ISBN: 0692874992
ISBN 13: 9780692874998

CHAPTER ONE

I turned eighteen and thought I was a man. I had heard my pa and my grandpa talk about what it was like to go out and build their own ranches in the old days. I decided that even though my pa had the W-H ranch and Grandpa had the Tumbling C, I wanted to go out on my own. Of course now a-days they made a lot more money selling oil than they did raising cattle. Pa wanted me to learn the oil business, so I worked on the drilling rigs last summer. I liked the rough necks that ran the rigs, but I still would rather work cattle.

I knew Pa had a dream of me going off to college and coming back to work for him and someday take over when he retired. I sure didn't want to disappoint him but I just couldn't stomach the idea of taking charity. I wanted to follow my dream like he and Grandpa had done.

I wanted to make it on my own. If I failed, I would come home with my tail between my legs or they would bury me on some lonesome prairie but I had it in my mind that I had to test my mettle, just like they had. I had two sisters, one of their husbands could work for dad and grandpa.

I remember when I was only about ten years old my pa told me, "Billy Joe, you're ten years old, it's time you learned to handle a six-shooter. Now watch me. fix your eye on what you're shooting at."

In one smooth fast fluid motion his right hand slipped the six-shooter out of the leather holster, and as it was coming out of the holster, his thumb pulled back the hammer. As soon as the six-shooter leveled, with his index finger curled around the trigger. When his thumb released the hammer, seventeen inches of flame and smoke erupted from the barrel and a tremendous explosion stung my young ears.

"Son, in a few years I hope you won't need to carry one of these everywhere you go, but in this day and time you better have a gun and you better know how to use it. Billy Joe, a gun is a tool, like a hammer or saw, it's designed to do a job. It is not a toy to be played with. I'm going to teach you how, because this gun, if handled properly, may someday save your life or the life of your mother or one of your sisters. There are a lot of renegades about and I can't always be with you or always be here to protect them. Do you want to learn?"

"Yes sir."

"I had this belt and holster made to fit you. This is a forty-four caliber Smith and Wesson. It is a very powerful weapon. At first it'll feel heavy and awkward, I want you and I to practice with it every evening for the next month. By the end of the month it will feel natural for you to draw and fire it in one motion. Speed is not as important as being accurate. In most gun fights the first shot misses. Make sure your first shot does not. Here try it on. Right now it's not loaded. I want you to get used to the feel and weight of the weapon."

Billy Joe thought back to that day his father started teaching him how to use a gun. Every evening after supper we would walk out behind the barn and practice for an hour. At first dad had me drawing the gun and pointing it at a target over and over again.

Then he would have me draw the gun, squeeze the trigger and drop the hammer in the same motion. He explained, "If you pull the trigger after you have the gun level, you'll pull the barrel off the target. Squeeze the trigger down as you are lifting the gun out of the holster and cock the hammer, then when you drop the hammer it's pointed right at the thing you are shooting at."

After a few weeks, I noticed the gun felt different when he handed it to me. I must have looked at it then looked at him.

"It feels, heavier doesn't it?"

"Yes sir."

"That's because it's loaded. I want you to do exactly like you've been doing, except this time make sure you've got a good grip on the pistol, 'cause when you drop that hammer, it's going to fire."

Boy, did I feel big as I strapped on that fully loaded forty-four. I'm sure I swaggered a little when I pulled the buckle tight around my waist. I sauntered up to the line we had made for me to stand on, when I was practicing. I was imagining that little ole sapling tree was a full-fledged bank robber coming in to rob the bank as I went in to make a deposit for pa. Of course, Pa had never let me make a deposit but that didn't matter. As smooth as greased lightning I whipped that six-shooter out of its holster and dropped the hammer on that bad dude.

Oh, my gosh the whole world exploded. Sixteen inches of fire and smoke shot out of the end of that ole six-shooter. The sapling split right down the middle. My ears drums felt like they busted. My right hand stung like a dozen wasps had hit it at the same time. I ducked as the barrel of that six-shooter flew over my right shoulder and landed in the dirt about twenty feet behind me. Tears were running down my face and then I realized something else…I had wet my pants.

Pa calmly walked over and picked up the six-shooter, took out his handkerchief and wiped the dirt off of it then said, "Son, I think that's enough lessons for today."

I was mortified, I ran back to the house as fast as my two feet could go to get me some clean clothes. It was hard trying to run straddle-legged so the wet jeans didn't touch my legs. I was praying nobody saw me before I got in the house. One thing I was sure of, I was never going to be a gun fighter if this happened every time I shot my gun. In fact I never wanted to see that thing again. What if I did wet my pants every time I shot it?

The next day Pa said, "Billy Joe remember I told you to get a good grip on the six-shooter."

"Yes sir."

"What did you learn yesterday?"

"That I don't ever want to shoot a gun again."

"That's a lesson I don't ever want you to forget. Guns are not a toy. No decent man wants to kill another. However, there are a lot of renegades running around that think it makes them feel important to be able to use a gun to take whatever they want. That's why you have-ta learn how to use a gun properly. I made a mistake when we started, I started you with the forty-four. In a way I'm glad. At least you weren't hurt and it taught you a lesson that I could never have taught you about what a fearful thing a gun really is. We're going to go out there and try it again today. Here's a smaller gun, this is a thirty-eight. It'll still need to be held in a firm grip. It's not as powerful as the forty-four but it's still a powerful weapon. This time make sure that you've got a firm grip on it before you drop the hammer."

I was shakin' like I had the palsy when I lifted that cannon out of its holster. I don't know which came first me squeezing my eyes shut or me squeezing the trigger. When the hammer dropped, that gun made a powerful loud bang. When I opened my eyes, I was still holding the gun in my hand but I had completely missed the new sapling tree that we had picked out. I was scared to look down at my pants. I let my breath out when I saw that I hadn't wet my pants.

"Billy Joe that was good, you held on to the six-shooter. Now this time try to keep your eyes open."

By the end of the month I had filled that ole sapling so full of lead that if somebody ever cuts it down, it'll weigh a ton.

After practice one day I stood and looked at the six-shooter I held in my hand and wondered if I would ever be forced to use it.

CHAPTER TWO

Now everybody who knows the family knows that my real mother was a real pretty lady named Mattie Ann and she died when I was born. My Aunt Sally Jo took me to raise like I was her own. Then after a while my Pa, Sam, married Sally Jo, so I took to calling her mama. She's the only mama I've ever known. Then she and Papa had two more kids. I was some put out when the second one turned out to be another little sister. Cause I surely wanted a little brother to play with.

Sisters are alright but you can't chase rabbits, and chuck rocks at hawks and crows, like you could with a brother.

When I turned sixteen pa put me to working on one of the oil drilling rigs. He said he wanted me to learn the family business from the ground up. I learned real quick, if you didn't pay attention around all that machinery you could get 'ground up' real fast.

I had been helping Juan and Russ around the cattle ever since my head was taller than the bottom of a stirrup. So, this year I told Pa I wanted to learn the cattle side of the family business.

After my seventeenth birthday Pa put me to working full time for Juan. I'll say this much for ole Juan, didn't care who my daddy was he expected me to pull my weight.

That's why I happened to be off in the northwest section hunting strays when I topped a ridge and pulled up. I could see Curtis, one of the hands, down at the bottom of the rise and three tough looking hombres had him boxed in. I couldn't hear what was being said but it sure looked like trouble to me. The way those hombres were spaced around him looked like real trouble. One was sitting on a horse about ten yards in front of Curtis. One was about ten yards on the east side of ole Curtis and the other one was off Curtis's left flank about ten yards. That put this one behind Curtis.

I had shot targets with Curtis enough to know he was some shakes with that six-shooter but there was no way he was gonna get all three of these guys if lead started flying. So I raked the spurs on the flank of ole B.J. and we went flying down that grassy hill like the devil was behind us with a fiery pitch fork.

We called my horse B.J., which stood for Buck Junior. My daddy had a horse named Buck that was his favorite horse until a rattlesnake bit the horse and daddy had to shoot him. Then a few weeks later one of the mares dropped a colt that looked just like ole Buck, so pa named him Buck Junior. I just shortened it to B.J. Those three hombres were so intent on Curtis that they didn't even hear me and B.J. come down the grassy hill until I was right on 'em.

I heard one of them say, "I don't like you, mister big mouth. You don't tell us where to ride."

"You're on W-H land and you got no business here. So I'm ordering you off." Curtis said.

"I think it's about time that somebody taught you W-H hands a lesson, so if I put six holes in you maybe the rest of 'em will learn a lesson."

One of the others said, "Let's hang him from that cottonwood and leave him swinging."

I had slowed my wild charge down the hill to a walk the last fifty yards. Now I was off the left shoulder of the guy who was off Curtis's left shoulder.

I just levered a round into my Winchester 30-30. Now there ain't a cowhand on the range that don't know that sound. I saw the guy in front of me stiffen like he had been hit with a cattle prod.

"Fellows, I don't know what this is all about but if you want to start the dance I just bought a ticket." I said.

The guy across from me looked startled when I declared myself. Then he said, "Hell, you ain't nothing but a kid."

"That may be true but this Winchester I'm holding is full grown. If you start anything this guy here in the plaid shirt better be prepared to meet his maker 'cause I'm gonna cut his spine right in two with this 30-30."

I swear you could see sweat popping out on the back of that dude's neck that had his back to me. So, I said, "What's it gonna be boys. You can reach down real easy and unbuckle them gun belts and let them fall or me and Curtis can start emptying saddles?"

The one on the east side of Curtis said, "I ain't takin' my gun off for nobody, especially some snot nosed kid." He did the dumbest thing a man can do. He jerked his six-shooter out of his holster. A 30-30 slug slapped him off the back of his horse.

Curtis whipped out his six-shooter a second before the man in front of him did and shot that man right through the brisket. The man in the plaid shirt threw both hands straight up to the sky, saying, "Don't shoot, it was Samson's idea. I was just riding along."

I held the rifle on him and aid, "Curtis take his gun."

"Now mister, turn around and look at me. My name is Billy Joe McClanton. I'm Sam McClanton's boy. So, tell me what you three were doing on my daddy's land. Don't lie and tell me you were just passing through, I ain't buying it."

CHAPTER THREE

S ally Jo looked at her two daughters and thought, *I am the most blessed woman in the world. I am married to the finest man God ever put on the earth, I have a son who is the spitting image of his father, and two beautiful little girls that are growing up too fast. Caroline will be thirteen her next birthday and Mattie will be ten. It just doesn't seem possible that they could all be gone in the next few years.*

Then she shuddered when she remembered Sam had been teaching Billy Joe how to shoot. Sam had said, "In these times Billy Joe must know how to handle a gun, there are too many outlaws and cutthroats still out there." That thought terrified the mother in her. She was sitting at the table so she pulled her Bible over to her and as she flipped it open, it opened to Psalms 41:2. When she read it she stopped and read it again. It said, "The LORD will protect him and keep him alive."

Sally Jo bowed her head and said, *"Lord, forgive me for not trusting you more. I love my family and you know we live in hard violent times. I can't protect them, so I trust you to do it. Thank you for sending this message to me today. Of all the verses in your Bible you made it open to that one. Thank you. In Jesus name. Amen"*

Sally Jo took the hem of her apron and wiped the tears from her eyes. A smile played across her face as she looked at the girls across the room, Caroline was knitting and Mattie was reading a book. Then she thought back to the day she had married Sam and little Billy Joe. The smile widened at the thought, I remember standing up there in front of the preacher and seeing Sam standing there with Billie Joe beside him and I thought, yes, I get them both with this ceremony.

CHAPTER FOUR

When that man in the plaid shirt turned around to face me he looked to be about twenty-five and plenty scared. He was scared because he knew that cattle rustling was still a hanging offence in Texas.

He licked his dry lips and stammered, "Samson said your Pa had so much money from the oil wells he wouldn't miss a hundred head of cattle and we could get a good price for 'em, but we never stole any of 'em."

"Mister, what's your name?"

"Everybody calls me Spike."

"Okay Spike." Pointing to the man Curtis had shot, "What's his handle?"

"Zack."

"And the one over there?"

"Turley."

"You can put your hands down. Now get down off that horse and get that trash off my land. Load both of them back on their horses and get off W-H land and if I ever see you here again I won't ask any questions, I'll just start shootin'. You got it?"

"Curtis you collect all the guns off them two bodies, before he loads 'em up."

I sat there on B.J. with the hammer pulled back on the Winchester just in case that dude decided to be stupid. He didn't, he suddenly had a bolt of smarts. When he got his loads secured he climbed up on his bronc and lit out of there.

Curtis walked over to stand beside my stirrup, "Boy was I glad to see you. I saw you out of the corner of my eye coming down that hill. I knew they hadn't noticed you coming so I kept them talking until you jacked that shell into the 30-30. If you had ridden up behind that old boy and blowed a bugle you wouldn't have startled him anymore."

"How did you know they were up to no good?"

"Just the way they were sneaking around and eye balling the cattle. They stayed off the ridge and were working their way down the hollows. It just didn't look right so I rode up on 'em and told 'em this was private property and they needed to move on. Then the one you shot started talking tough and they separated so that I couldn't get a shot at more than one before the other two filled me full of lead."

"Well two of 'em won't be causing any more trouble. I hope the one we let go will see the error of his ways and we won't see any more of him."

Riding back side by side toward the ranch house Curtis said, "Billy Joe, you are a might young but you'll do to ride the river with. That was quick action and good thinking back there. I owe you, 'cause that dude you shot was planning on killing me. I knew it. He just wanted to watch me sweat a little first."

"When we get back to the house, we'll call the sheriff and report what happened. I don't expect any trouble because they shucked iron first, plus Spike admitted they were out to rustle cattle."

When I came down to the barn the next day, Curtis had already told all the other hands about the shoot out, and of course each time he told it, it got hairier and hairier.

Mid-morning, I was forking hay to the horses in the corral when Pa walked up and hooked his boot heel on the lowest rail. "I hear tell you and Curtis had a run in with some would-be rustlers yesterday."

"Yes sir. We had a little."

"Tell me about it."

So, I stood there leaning on the corral bars and told him the whole story. He stood and looked at me a moment then said, "Son, I taught you how to shoot straight. Now I reckon it's time to teach you how to shoot fast and straight. Go up there to the house and get about three boxes of shells for that forty-four you're wearing and meet me down in that gulley behind the horse barn."

All afternoon Pa had me doing the craziest thing. He picked up a pretty good sized rock and he would hold it at varying heights and angles from me and tell me to shoot that rock before it hit the ground.

I got so tired of shootin' at rocks, but in a few weeks I was busting nine out of ten of 'em every time.

After I'd shot up about ten boxes of bullets one day I looked up and saw pa standing up there at the top of the gulley watching me.

"Son you have a natural dexterity that's as good as I've ever seen. I just stood here and watched you drop ten straight rocks out of your right hand then reach down and pull out your pistol and bust every one of them before they hit the ground. That's amazingly fast and accurate. That skill can save your life or the life of someone you love. It can also be a curse of gigantic proportions if you don't handle it well. You don't need to be showing off how fast you are to anybody because there are still crazy men out there that will challenge you to prove they are faster."

"Yes sir."

"Billy Joe, that's why I had you practicing down here in the gulley so even the hands couldn't watch you. I already knew how fast your hands moved and how accurate your aim is. As you know a gun is a fearsome thing. There are two kinds of men out there.

Most men will freeze and do nothing when they face a gun fight. You have already proved you'll react if you must."

"The other kind are men who get killing in their blood and if they hear a man is fast with his gun, they will want to kill him just to prove they can. I'm not concerned with you becoming one of them. However, I don't want them coming after you."

CHAPTER FIVE

The morning after I turned eighteen, B.J. and I were riding and topped a ridge and saw a whole bunch of people, some on horses, some in wagons, even one on a bicycle cutting across our land headed north. I just sat and watched them for a few minutes and thought, now that is strange. Most time when we see travelers they are on the main road headed west. So I rode down to talk to some of them.

I pulled up next to a family in a wagon. "Howdy."

"Howdy son what can I do fer ye?"

"I'm Billy Joe McClanton. My daddy owns this land. He won't care if you're cutting across it but I'm just curious where everybody's going. We don't usually see travelers going north."

"They're giving away free land up in the Oklahoma Territory, so we're headed up there to claim some of it."

"Really." Then I spied something else. The prettiest girl about my age stood up behind the wagon seat and looked at me. She had long black hair and the prettiest dark brown eyes I'd ever seen.

She said, "And who are you?"

I whipped off my hat and said, "Billy Joe McClanton ma'am."

"Are you trying to be a robber or a beggar?"

The man on the wagon seat said, "Mary Beth, watch your manners. This young man says his daddy owns this land we're passing through and he's just being neighborly. Son, my name is Charles Carpenter, and this is my daughter Mary Beth."

"Glad to meet ya. Do you mind if I ride along with you a ways, I would like to know some more about this land deal?"

He snapped the reins on the back of the mules and started moving forward. "Suit yourself. If your daddy owns all this land why do you need any more?"

"Sir that's just it. My daddy owns all this land and my grandpa owns all the land east of here but I don't want to live off what they've done. I want to build something that's mine. Something I built with my own labor and sweat."

Now I saw that Mary Beth had eased around the end of the wagon seat and was sitting up there with her papa. She was wearing a plain gingham dress but I ain't never seen anybody looking that pretty in a gingham dress before. She didn't say anymore she just listened as her pa told me about how the land give away was supposed to work.

I rode alongside them for another mile then said, "Well I guess I better get back to work. Mr. Carpenter, I hope you get some good land. I tipped my hat to Mary Beth and said, "If I come up there and get some land, maybe we can be neighbors."

⊷⊶ ⊷⊶

Joe Carville, loaded his pipe and taking tongs he lifted a hot coal from the fireplace to light it. He walked out on the back porch to watch the sun set and smoke his pipe. Rosa appeared by his elbow with a cup of hot coffee.

"Rosa, why don't you get you a cup of coffee and join me. Let's watch this sunset and talk a minute, I've got something on my mind."

Rosa returned in a moment with a steaming cup of coffee for herself. As soon as she sat down Joe Carville said, "Rosa we have worked together for a long time. In fact you raised Mattie Ann after we lost her mother, and you did a fine job."

"No Mr. Joe all I did was feed her and do my best to keep her cleaned up. I swear that child could get in more mud than any child I ever seen. If there was one mud puddle in a hundred sections, I swear she'd find it"

Joe Carville chuckled and said, "Yeah, when she was little you'd have her all shined up for church and if you looked off for a minute she'd be in the hog pen."

Now they were both laughing. "You know Mr. Joe, she turned out to be a fine lady. She loved Sam McClanton and he loved her just as much. "

"Yeah, she did and you're right he loved her just as much. Together they brought a fine boy into this world."

"Mama-mia they sure did. That Billy Joe would look at you with them big blue eyes and melt your heart."

"I still ache when I think about losing Mattie Ann, but I praise God every day for Sally Jo. She's doing a wonderful job raising all three of those kids. Rosa, have you ever had a bad feeling that something is fixin' to happen and you can't do anything to stop it?"

"Like I started to say Mr. Joe, that Mattie Ann loved her Papa. Her eyes would light up when she heard your horse come into the yard. I never did understand how she could tell your horse from the others but she could."

"I guess I'm just getting' old, but lately I can't shake this feeling."

"To answer your question, the answer is yes. The old folks used to call it the second sight. Every time I get to feeling that way I go get my Bible. That Bible is sure a comfort 'cause this much I know death is certain, and life is not. So I read where if we trust in God no matter what happens he is still watching over us. Look at it this way, we lost Mattie Ann which is terrible bad, but we got Sally

Jo and Billy Joe which is awfully good. And I know Mattie Ann's loving the place she's at right now and when we get there the renegades first people we're gonna see waitin' to welcome us home is gonna be Mattie Ann, and her mama."

"Rosa, I sure hope you're right. I look forward to seeing Mattie Ann and her mother someday. I just pray that I'm not overlooking something that I could be doing right now to protect Sally Jo and those three kids that I haven't thought of yet."

CHAPTER SIX

After supper pa sat back in his chair and said, "Billy Joe, they've got a new college that just opened up last year called Texas Agricultural and Mechanical College. I've checked into it and they've got some fine professors. They imported them from Georgia, South Carolina, and even as far away as England. You know soon it'll be 1900. The world as we know it is changing. A man is gonna need education if he is gonna make anything of himself. Sally Jo and I would like to see you go down there and get you the best education you can get and then come back here and help me run this place for a few years then when I get older you can take over."

"You mean they've got a college right here in Texas. I won't have-ta go off to Boston or someplace to go to college?"

Sally Jo said, "It is only about two-hundred miles to this college. It's a lot closer than the one back east."

Everybody was quiet for a minute, each one thinking over this new development. Sam said, "It is closer but it'll take about ten days to get there to this Texas Agricultural and Mechanical College on horseback and only two days to get to Boston on the train."

"That's true Pa, but how long would it take if we bought one of those automobiles? I hear they can go thirty miles in an hour."

"I've been thinking about that ever since we got the tractor. In fact, in the paper there are pictures of about twenty different cars being produced right now. There's the Daimler car, Ford cars and somebody named Rumson Olds has come out with a new one. The one I think I like best is called a Packard. There are two or three that run off steam. Of course we are in the oil and gas business so I'm not going to buy a car that runs on steam."

Sally Jo laughed and said, "You better not. Your neighbors will stand on the side of the road and throw rocks at you. Seriously, those things scare me. They look so dangerous. I'm scared one of you will get hurt in one of those things."

"Honey, let me remind you, you said the same thing about a train."

"Well, Pa, I appreciate what you're thinking and the idea of owning one of them run-abouts is real exciting. However, I met some people today that told me they're going to be giving away free land over in the Oklahoma Territory. I know you would like for me to go to this college and then come back here and work for you. What I want to do is go up there to the Oklahoma Territory and get some land of my own. I want to do what you and grandpa have done, I want to build something myself."

"Son I appreciate what you're feeling, but there is no need for you to go through what your mama and I went through. It might look romantic and adventurous to you but let me tell you it was hard. That's why we did it, so you and your sisters wouldn't have to. You need to go to college and learn all of them new things they're teaching and come back and help me run this thing we've built."

"Pa, I gotta try it my way. You know I love you and mama, but I've gotta try it my way."

Sam started to say something and Sally Jo put her hand on his arm and said, "Billy Joe you and your daddy are just alike. That's why I love you both so much, you're strong willed men, of great character. Will you promise me something?"

"What?"

"Will you promise me that if you go up there in Oklahoma Territory that you'll be careful and if it doesn't work out in two years you'll come back and go to the college?"

"Mama, you know I'll be careful, I'm not going to go off half-cocked. Two years is a mighty short time."

"Remember it didn't take your pa but one season to sell enough horses to know the ranch was going to work."

"Son, before you make a promise you can't keep., I want you to ride over to your grandpa's and talk to him. Make your decision as to what you really want to do after you talk to him. Then you can come back and tell me and your mom what you've decided. Will you at least do that for me?"

I wanted to go out on my own but all I could think about was Mary Beth. Of course, I had no idea how I would find her if I went to the Oklahoma Territory. It was a big territory and they could have settled anywhere.

"Yes sir, I'll ride over to the Tumbling *C* tomorrow and talk to grandpa."

"There's one thing more. I 've got a gift for you." She walked to the mantel and picked up a package wrapped in brown mailing paper and handed it to him.

"What's this?"

"Open it."

Billy Joe opened a beautiful leather bound Bible.

"I want you to take this with you everywhere you go."

Billy Joe hugged her and said, "Mama I promise I will."

Sam kissed his wife goodbye and climbed up in the buggy. Glancing at the back seat said, "Okay girls are we ready for another fun day at school?"

"Sure Papa, but why isn't Billy Joe taking us to school?"

"He wanted to go look at some wild horses. He saw one he really liked the other day."

Caroline said, "All the girls will be disappointed. I think every girl in school has a crush on our brother."

"If he wasn't my brother I think I would have a crush on him too." Mattie giggled.

"Okay you two. You're way too young to be having a crush on any boy. You have to wait until you're at least thirty."

"Papa, you forget I'll be thirteen in a month. Mattie is only ten so she's too young."

Sam said with a grin, "Your Pa thinks both of you are too young, you're still my little girls."

"How old was mama when you met her?"

"Hmmm, let me think. I think she was about forty."

Giggling came out of the back of the buggy. "That's not true, she's not even forty yet." Caroline said.

"Papa when are you going to buy one of those automobiles like the Hightower's have?" Mattie said.

"What's wrong with old Nell? She gets us where we want to go alright."

They both groaned and said, "Papa, a horse and buggy is so old fashioned. All of the other families are getting automobiles."

Sam laughed and said. "All of the other families? I have only seen one other family with an automobile in the whole area."

"Well their girls brag about it all the time. So you need to get one too."

"I'll tell you what, you get your mother to agree and I'll buy us an automobile."

"Really, would you do that?"

"You bet."

Sam looked back at his two princesses', and thought *what a blessed man I am.* He felt his shirt buttons stretch tight when he thought about his family, Sally Jo, Billy Joe, these two beautiful young ladies in his carriage.

Sam tipped his hat to a family in a wagon headed in the opposite direction.

⊨⊰ ⊱⊨

When Joe Carville came in for breakfast Russ and Rosa were both standing there in the kitchen looking like two raccoons peeping out from under the back porch. All Joe could see was four big eyes and rows of teeth, they were both smiling so.

Rosa spoke first, "Mr. Joe we've got something to tell you. I'll let Russ do the telling."

"What're you two up to?"

"Well boss, Rosa and me are gonna get married. You see I've been eatin' her cookin' so long I decided one of us had to marry her so nobody could come along and steal our cook. I decided you wasn't gonna do it so I asked her to marry me."

Joe looked at Rosa and then back at Russ and said, "I'll be dad-gum. That is the darndest thing I ever heard. Now I'm not fixing to lose both of you am I?"

"No sir, I thought maybe you could sell Rosa and me a little piece of land so I can build us a small house."

"No I won't sell you a piece of land. I'll give you a piece of land and me and the boys will help you build a house on it. When do you want to get married?"

"Not till we get the house built."

Joe reached over and hugged Rosa and said, "You better get Sally Jo over here to help make you a wedding dress 'cause we are fixin' to build a house."

23

About that time, Billy Joe walked in the back door. Everybody was standing there grinning. I stopped and looked at them then said, "What did I just miss?"

Grandpa said, "Rosa and Russ are gonna get married."

"Get out-a-here. Are you kidding me?"

"No Billy Joe, I asked Rosa to marry me and she said yes."

⊷⊷ ⊶⊶

The next morning at breakfast Sam said, "Billy Joe if you're bound and determined to have a look at this Oklahoma thing, when are you thinking about going?"

"Well pa, the folks I talked to said that the giveaway will be on the 15th of next month so I'm thinking I need to go on up there and scout out the land I want to get and get registered. Only those who are preregistered will be allowed to get any land."

"How are they supposed to give away the land?"

"The way I understand it, is on the 15th of next month at high-noon they will fire a cannon and then it's a race. Each farm or city block for towns will have a flag with a number on it. When you register they give you a flag. If you get there first and pull up the numbered flag and put your flag, in its place you own the land. Then over the next thirty days or so the army will come around and record the name of each land owner."

"Well that seems simple enough. I guess you'll need a fast horse, so you can get there first."

"Pa, I suspect there will be a lot of fast horses up there that day."

"I'll bet your right. If I was you I'd pick out three good pieces of land and if somebody beat me to the first one, I'd high-tail it to the next one."

"It's a two-day ride to the border of the Oklahoma Territory so I want to leave this morning. I'll go right to the fort and register then I'll meander around and look over the land. I not only want

24

to look at the plot, I want to pick out the best route from the starting point to the flag on the land I like."

"Son you be careful 'cause land is money and anytime there's money involved, there will be thieves and cut-throats out to get it from the people who earned it."

An hour later Sam and the girls climbed in the buggy headed for school again, and Billy Joe, riding BJ and leading a pack horse, struck off north to the Oklahoma Territory.

CHAPTER SEVEN

R uss and Rosa stood looking at a plot of ground with big oak trees and backing up to the creek. "Rosa, we could build the house right here. The front porch would be under the shade of that big oak, it would be facing south so the north wind wouldn't blow in every time you open the door."

"Russ honey, think about it, we will be going in and out of the back door more than the front door. The barns, garden, well and everything would be on the north side of the house. So that's the door we will be going in and out of the most."

"Hmmmm, let me think about that a minute. I'll tell you what we can do. We'll build a big back porch on the house. I'll get a bunch of that canvas like they cover wagons with and attach it to the eaves of the porch. In the winter we'll tack them down and keep the wind out. Then in the summer we'll roll them up so the breeze can come in."

"Mr. Engineer, are you gonna put running water in my kitchen like Sally Jo's got?"

"We won't have a running spring next to the house like they do so what I'll do is put a well with a pump on it on the back porch.

That way my little Rosa won't have to go outside to get water. That's the best I can do right now."

"Russ you know I was just teasing you. That porch idea is a good idea though. I think this spot is great. It's a short walk over to Mr. C's house and the bunk house."

"Rosa, we both know what a swell guy he is, to give us the land and allow me to cut the timber off his land to build with. A better boss would be hard to find."

He put his arm around her ample waist and said, "You know I look forward to being your husband. I'll do my best to be a good one."

"Cut your Irish blarney. I've been training you for twenty years."

"Oh you have, have you? Well I'll confess it was your cornbread that did it."

CHAPTER EIGHT

S ally Jo stood with tears in her eyes as she watched her family growing apart. Sam was taking the girls off to school and Billy Joe going off into who knows what. She bowed her head and said, *"Father God, please watch over my family, please watch over my girls until they return home this evening. May they have a pleasant day at school, and their minds be open to learning today. Please watch over Sam as he goes about his business today, he is our rock and we thank you for this wonderful man.*

Oh God I especially pray for Billy Joe, I know every mother has to watch her son leave home and become a man, but it seems so soon. I am not ready for him to go out into the big wide cruel world. I put my faith in you to watch over him and protect him from evil.

I beg these things in your son's name. Amen."

⊷⊶

As the buggy dropped down into the dried creek bed they were temporarily out of sight from anyone in town. Before Sam could take the thong off his six-gun, three rough looking characters appeared from around the bend in the creek with their guns drawn.

"Okay old man, we need for you to hand over that money pouch we know you've got on ya."

One of the thugs said, "Look at them purty little lassies. I think I'll just climb in that buggy and get me a kiss."

He rode up beside the buggy and when he tried to step out of his saddle and into the buggy a black snake whip snapped around his neck.

He screamed and tried to claw the rawhide leather whip off his neck and Sam jerked hard on the whip handle snatching him into the buggy. A big barrel forty-four magically appeared in Sam's right hand. Sam tightened the grip of the whip cord around the man's neck. Now he was turning blue.

"Alright boys either you drop them guns right now or this man dies and then I'm gonna unleash these bad forty-fours. You see you have a problem if you try to shoot me you're probably gonna hit him first and if I don't let him get some air pretty soon he's gone anyway. So, either drop them guns or at least two of you are gonna die, him and at least one of you." They heard the unmistakable sound of the hammer cocking on Sam's forty-four, "DROP THEM NOW!"

Two gun belts dropped in the dirt. Sam released the whip from around the thug's throat. "Okay you knuckle heads, tell me your names and do it now."

"What if I don't want to tell you my name?" He eared back the hammer on the forty-four. "Then you'll be buried without any name on your cross."

"Man you can't shoot us we ain't done nothing'. Snake's the one who bothered the ladies."

"Is his name Snake?"

"Yeah, Snake Calvert." You could see sweat popping out all over them. They wanted to wheel their horses around and make a break for it but they knew that long barrel forty-four would hit them before they could get away.

"Okay his name is Snake Calvert, now tell me your names. NOW!"

Sam pointed the six-shooter right in the face of one of the outlaws and said, "What do they call you?"

The man's Adams apple bobbed up and down as he swallowed hard and said, "Dee, everybody calls me Dee."

Sam fired one round that barely missed his ear and said, "What does your mama call ya?"

"Leroy."

"Chuck Swenson, that's my name." The third man volunteered.

Then Sam calmly climbed down and walked around the buggy. The thug was leaning against the side of the buggy with his hands around his throat gasping to regain his breath.

Sam looked at the man leaning against the wagon wheel still trying to get all his breath back and said, "You tried to molest one of my girls." Then Sam proceeded to whip the man until his shirt was all in tatters and red whelps covered his whole upper body.

Looking straight at the other two Sam said, "You better get this straight and tell all of your buddies. If anyone ever bothers one of these girls I will beat him to death with this whip." Turning back to the man he had just whipped he said, "Snake, you get on that horse and ride out of the state of Texas because if I ever see you again, today was just a little sample. I hope you learned your lesson. In fact don't ever let me see any of you again. Now, all three of you get out of my sight."

He recoiled his whip and climbed back in the buggy. "Girls if you ever see any one of those men again, I want you to tell me."

⛓✦✦⛓

Billy Joe rode up a dry cut in the hills until he found a small clear stream with some good grass to picket the horses on. He stripped off the saddles and grabbed a hand full of dried grass and rubbed down each horse, led them to water, then picketed them for the night.

Any cowman knew that first you saw after your horses before you made do for yourself. Billy Joe took his coffee pot and filled it with sparkling cold, clean creek water. Warmed up his frying pan and sliced off several slices of bacon. Walked back down to the creek with a cooking pan and dipped it full of water. He shook in a few ounces of the biscuit flour. Then took out his bowie knife and used it to stir the flour and water until it was mixed well.

Billy Joe leaned back against his saddle and breathed in the wonderful smell of bacon frying and biscuits rising in the pan. He watched a big silver moon as it crept higher in the night sky.

He always marveled at the number of stars in the vast black expanse stretching over head. He had camped out many nights on the range but he had to admit that it felt different to be sleeping on ground that was not owned by his dad. It was so peaceful listening to the horses cropping grass, the bacon sizzling in the frying pan, and a night bird calling in the trees.

Soon it was like a symphony, the lonesome sound of the dove, chirp of the crickets, a coyote serenading the moon and the deep base sound of a big frog by the creek.

His mind was busy thinking, 'I'll find the Carpenters and get me a place close to theirs because that Mary Beth is the prettiest gal I have ever seen."

After eating his biscuits and bacon and cleaning his utensils he rolled up in his blanket with his six-shooter by his side and dreamed of Mary Beth Carpenter.

CHAPTER NINE

J oe Carville's tractor had a big flywheel on the side of the motor that you could wrap a big leather belt around and he had bought a large saw blade. By starting the motor on the tractor the flywheel would run the belt that spun the large circular saw blade. That made it a lot easier than when they ran it with the steam engine, you didn't have to worry about keeping the fire going or the boiler full of water, as long as that tractor had gas in it, it would keep running. It was amazing you could split large tree trunks into building planks as fast as you could push them through the mill. In one day Russ and the boys had enough lumber cut to frame the entire house.

"Russ, stack the lumber you have cut in the big barn and let it cure for a few days. If you leave it outside your boards will be all warped and crooked. We'll move those cows up to the north range and take time to brand all the calves, by the time we get through your lumber should be ready for you guys to start framing."

⊫⟨+ +⟩⊨

Charles Carpenter was talking to some of the soldiers, "Where do you think a man will find the best farm land?"

"Sir we have patrolled all over this territory and the best farm land I've seen is up in the northern part."

Another soldier spoke up and said, "They will be letting people in from the Kansas side and the Texas side. The crowds are gonna be a lot bigger coming from the Texas side. So a fella's got a lot less competition coming from the Kansas side. It's gonna be a mad rush from the Texas side."

"Yeah, there are over a hundred thousand people signed up for this and when they fire that cannon at noon you're going to have a hundred thousand horses and wagons galloping across the prairie. I expect they'll get a lot of people killed that day."

Charles Carpenter stood pondering this information for a few seconds then said, "Sergeant, why do you say a bunch of farmers are gonna get killed?"

"Cause anytime you got something for free, people go crazy. Especially, if you've got something as valuable as land that you are giving away. If you've got that many horses racing across unfamiliar ground some horse is gonna fall and somebody is gonna get trampled to death."

Another soldier said, "And everybody out there will be packing guns. If two guys are trying for the same flag, look out."

When Charles Carpenter got back to his wagon he said, "Mary Beth, pack up the cooking stuff we are moving up to the northern part."

"Why pa? This looks like some pretty good land right around here."

"Those soldier boys told me some things that makes me think we need to move farther north."

She thought, *oh well that handsome guy from Texas probably ain't gonna come anyway. No use sittin' around hoping.*

Two days later Billy Joe rode across the red river and up to the temporary registering station. He couldn't believe what his eyes were seeing. There must have been two hundred wagons and tents set up around the registering station. It was the biggest town he had ever seen and it wasn't even a town.

He walked into the tent and a man with a long black coat and mutton chop sideburns sat behind a table with two army officers on either side of him, "What cha need son?"

"Is this where I sign up to get some land?"

"This is where you register but there ain't no guarantee you are gonna get any land though."

"I heard the government was going to give away land up here."

"Oh they're gonna give it away that's for sure."

"Then why did you say there's no guarantee I was going to get any of it?"

An old army private that was way too old to be a private snarled, "This here's Mr. Ledbetter, he's the land agent for the Federal Government. I don't like your smart mouth, for two cents I'd knock you flat in the dirt then pick you up and throw you back across the Red River."

Billy Joe said, "Mr. Ledbetter, I meant no disrespect, I just don't understand what you are saying. As to this big blow-hard, if he thinks he can pick me up and throw me anywhere all he has got to do is try it."

The private started to step forward with his fist clenched. The man in the mutton chops said, "At ease private."

Then he turned to Billy Joe and said, "Son look out there at all those folks and there's more coming every day. All I'm saying is there ain't gonna be enough land to go around, there's more takers than there is land. The army's doing the best they can to keep everything under control. We've already had two killings this week, one was shot and the other was knifed. We've still got three more weeks to go. Step up here and write your name in this book if you can write. If you can't, make your mark and one of these fellows sitting here beside me will write you name down beside your mark."

"Sir, I can write my own name."

"Okay then write your name right here and I'll give you a copy of the rules."

Billy Joe wrote his name and received his copy of the rules. He wanted to say more to the big mouth private but decided to let it go. After he left the tent Billy Joe led his horses to the river and let them drink.

Sitting by his camp fire that night he read the rules given to him by the agent. In it he found that he was allowed to ride over the area and pick out the land he wanted, but he had to be back across the river before the 15th.

Next morning at first light he headed north to scout the land. He had asked around the camp last night about the Carpenters, several people remembered them being there but they were gone now. He thought *I guess Mr. Carpenter is doing the same thing, he's scouting the land and they'll be back here in time for the start.*

CHAPTER ELEVEN

Rosa walked through the house. It was beautiful. The guys had done a wonderful job, she loved the kitchen. Even if it would not get much use since most of their meals would still be eaten at Mr. C's house. As she moved into the parlor or main room she loved the big open fireplace. In her mind's eye she could see her and Russ snuggling up in front of a roaring fire on a winter night.

The floors gleamed, the men had sanded and polished the wood for the floors until the finish was like a mirror.

This time next week they would be married, and she would move all of her things over to this house. Her own home, what a wonderful feeling that thought brought.

◄═╫ ╫═►

Billy Joe rode north east from the sign-in, station toward the Davis Mountains. The land he rode through was miles and miles of gently rolling hills. He observed the land he was riding through. The grass was as tall as the bottom of his stirrup in places. Good rich looking farm land, but he wasn't looking to plant crops. He wasn't sure what he was looking for. What he was really looking for was Mary Beth Carpenter. He couldn't stop thinking about those big brown captivating eyes.

As the sun was setting he spotted a camp fire with several people around it.

"Hello the camp. Can company come in?"

"If you're peaceful come on. If you're not just know that six forty-fours are covering you."

A tall man in an old army hat stood as he rode up, "Howdy pilgrim are you out scoutin' land too?"

"Yes sir, my name is Billy Joe McClanton from down Cactus Tree area and I heard they was giving away land up this way."

One of the other men said, "They ain't givin' none of it away yet."

The tall man stuck out his hand, "Ruff Stubbs from Tennessee." Pointing to the man who had spoken up, "This is my brother, Luther and my son Joshua."

"I've got some bacon and beans; I'll be glad to pitch in on the grub for tonight." Billy Joe said.

"We done killed an antelope and got us a mulligan stew brewin' but you can always throw in some for breakfast if-n you want to throw down your bed roll."

It was peaceful sitting around the campfire drinking coffee and just yarning the hours away. Several times one of the men mentioned the fact there were no trees big enough to build with.

Luther said, "We'll just have to cut sod blocks and build sod houses until we get enough money to freight in some lumber for proper building."

"Shuuu, listen." Then they all heard horses walking in quiet like.

Each man reached down and slipped the thong off his six–shooter. Luke reached over and picked up an old Sharps 50 caliber.

When they were almost in the edge of the light one of the men on the horses spoke up. "Would you be sharing some of that stew, we ain't et nothing all day?"

Rather strange, they didn't hail the camp. They just rode in and demanded to be fed.

Three shifty looking characters stepped down and walked up to the fire. Ruff handed each one a tin plate and a spoon. "Dig in fellows, we ain't never turned a hungry man away with an empty belly."

They didn't even say thank you. What kind of dudes are these guys? They haven't even said their names. I'm leaving the thong off my six-shooter. I hope after they eat they'll move on. I don't trust these three at all.

One of the ruffian's kept looking out of the corner of his eye at Billy Joe, "Ain't I seen you someplace before?"

"I doubt it."

"Where you from?"

"Some place you're not."

"You got a smart mouth," and he started to jump up. One of his buddies pulled him back down.

"We'll be movin' on we've got some ground to cover."

One of them looked at Billy Joe and said, "We'll meet again." As lithe as a cat Billy Joe was on his feet, "If you've got a problem we can settle it right now. I'll unbuckle my gun belt when you do or we can cut loose right now. You call the tune, I'm ready to dance."

The other two looked around and realized that six more guns were pointing at them.

"Ah come on Snake, these folks let us eat their stew we don't want no trouble. Forget it kid he's just tired and irritable, come on Snake let's ride."

CHAPTER TEN

Russ heard a honking sound and looked up. "Look the geese are flying back north. I always think it is amazing how they always form a perfect "V" when they fly long distances."

"You know why they always fly in a "V"?" Joe Carville said.

"No."

"Each one parts the wind for the one behind him making it easier to fly long distances."

"How do they know which way is north?"

"I don't know, but even that is proof that God has designed everything to work as it does in nature." Russ said.

"You know Russ, I remember in Jeremiah about the eighth chapter it says, *Even the stork in the sky knows her appointed seasons, and the dove, the swift and the thrush observe the time of their migration.* "So, it isn't just ducks and geese that migrate."

"Oh well I don't know what makes them geese do what they do but I do know what makes that hay get in the barn, so let's go."

"Rosa, you're not going to bake your own wedding cake and you are not going to cook your own wedding supper. The reception after the ceremony is going to be at my house and the girls and I are going to do it."

Rosa laughed and said, "Listen here Miss Bossy. I'm the one who taught you how to cook."

"Yes, and you taught me well. So, it is settled, my girls and I are going to do the cooking on that day. Sam has a calf penned up and he has been grain feeding it for a month or more. The night before the wedding he will put it on the spit over the fire pit and start it to roasting. All you and Russ have to do is show up and it will all be done."

"I guess Mattie is gonna make some pies. I declare that child loves to make pies."

"Yes, and Caroline is going to help me decorate the cake. Wait until you see it."

"I love those girls like they was my own."

"Rosa, you are the only grandmother they have ever known. I know you told them to call you Aunt Rosa. Aunt or Grandmother, you know they both love you."

"Sally Jo, have you heard anything from Billy Joe?"

"No. I know that they do grow up and leave the nest but I still worry and I pray for him every day."

"Me too, I pray for all three of your kids every day. Billy Joe's a good boy, or man, it's just hard to think of him as a man. He'll be alright because he's a lot like his daddy and Sam has trained him well."

⋯

Billy Joe pulled out his tally book and marked off day four. Talking to his horses he said, "Well boys we only have ten more days until we've got to be back at the starting line. I still don't see what I'm looking for. I guess I don't see what I'm looking for because I don't know what I'm looking for exactly. I just know I haven't seen or heard anything about Mr. Carpenter and Mary Beth. I heard talk about a family that got robbed and the man was killed yesterday a few miles west of here, but they said the widow had two boys, so at least it wasn't the Carpenters."

On the morning of day nine, Billy Joe saddled up his horse and loaded his packhorse. It was then he discovered that he had lost the Bible his mother had given him. Frantically he looked through all his belongings, it was not there. He sat down and tried to re-member the last time he had seen it. He felt really bad because she had given it to him and he had promised he would always keep it with him.

He stood up and walked to the horses, "Well, boys which way are we going to go today? I think I see some taller hills on the eastern horizon. Why don't we head east and see what we find? Because tomorrow morning we have-ta head back to the starting line."

As he rode east he noticed that the hills were getting steeper and the trees more prolific. By sundown he was looking at a rath-er large hill or small mountain. Scouting the base of the hill he found a cleft that ran through it. Climbing to the top of the pass he was surprised to see a beautiful valley on the other side of the mountain. What really caught his attention was he found a rather large waterfall. Apparently, there was an active spring high up on the mountain that fed the stream that made a rapidly cascading waterfall on the western slope of the mountain. He didn't see it un-til he was almost on top of it because of the dense growth of trees. Looking closely, he found mostly Black Jack, Oak, and Elm trees. There were a few scattered Pine and Bois-d'arc trees, of course there were plenty of the ever present Cedars. The interesting thing was there was a survey flag at the entrance to the cut or cleft in the mountain but none on the eastern side of the pass. Talking to his horses again he said, "Boys, does that mean the free land stops here, or that the surveyors failed to climb up and look over the crest?"

Billy Joe pulled out his map of the land to be given away. He located the survey stake number on the map but it made no reference to the valley he saw from the crest. "Boys if a fellow got this entrance deeded to him he would control that valley too because there is no other way in that I can see. I'll bet most people are looking for land they can farm. There is no land that they can see from here that is farmable, so they may by pass this survey. This is the one I want. Jotting down the number on the survey stake and marking the spot on his map he headed back toward the starting location.

That night Billy Joe had an uneasy feeling. He didn't quite know why. He just did. It seemed today being the last day he had seen more undesirable characters racing around looking at survey stakes. He killed a jackrabbit and roasted it on a spit over his fire and washed it down with a cup of horseshoe coffee, he chuckled and said to himself, "Old cowhands always said if a horseshoe wouldn't float in your coffee, it wasn't strong enough."

As soon as he finished eating and banked the fire so it couldn't spread, he mounted back up and moved a quarter mile back in the hills, picketed his horses and made a dry camp.

During the night he woke when he heard shots being fired in the direction of his first camp. He looked up at the stars and determined it to be about 2:00 O'clock, rolled over and went back to sleep. Trusting his mustangs to warn him if anybody approached his camp.

When he saddled up and rode out he passed by his first camp from last night. He saw where three horses had ridden into the camp. Whoever came after him left the campsite in a mess. There was an empty whiskey bottle thrown on the ground, trash and litter was everywhere. "What kind of animals would leave a campsite looking like that? I'm glad I moved."

He was hoping to find the Carpenters when he got to the starting line. When he reached the starting point the army had pushed everybody back across the Red River. The line must have stretched for five miles along the south side of the river.

He saw every kind of conveyance, people on foot, people in wagons, on horseback, big wheel bicycles, on donkeys, two wheel carts, and even one dude on a unicycle. Billy Joe stared in wonder. He had never seen that many people in all his life.

It wasn't quite sundown as he rode along the line looking for Mary Beth and her father. They had to be here somewhere. He thought *well the land I want is over to the east so I will set up on the east end of this line and keep my eyes open for Mr. Carpenter. I sure hope they are alright, they have got to be here some place. Somebody had set a barrel of whiskey on the tailgate of a wagon and was selling liquor by the drink.*

When Billy Joe rode past a half drunk old army private saw him. "Hey there is that snot nose kid that the agent kept from getting a whooping'. Sonny boy your mama ain't here to protect ya now. I'm gonna drag you off that horse and whoop your tail."

Billy Joe looked and a bunch of half-drunk revelers were cheering the man on.

CHAPTER ELEVEN

S am walked out to check the horses one last time before turning in when he heard a horse coming at a full gallop. He stopped and instinctively lifted the thong that was holding his six-shooter in the holster.

One of the hands raced into the yard on a lathered up horse. "Sam we've had an accident at the Tumbling *C*. We need a doctor quick and we need some help getting some of them out."

Juan heard the horse race in and came out of the bunk house.

Sam wheeled around and said, "Juan send one of the boys to town and tell the doc to meet us at the Tumbling *C*. Get the rest of the guys in the saddle, let's go."

Sam ran back into the house and grabbed a jacket. Sally Jo looked up from cleaning the supper dishes and said, "Honey, what's the matter?"

"I don't know. A rider just raced in and said they had some kind of accident at the Tumbling *C* and they needed help."

"Sam tell one of the boys to get the buckboard out, I want to go. Rosa may need me."

Caroline walked in, "What's the matter?"

"We don't know. All we know is they have had some kind of accident at the Tumbling C and they are asking for our help."

"Is anybody hurt?"

"Yes. There must be because they asked us to send for the doctor."

"Me and Mattie want-ta go too if that's alright."

"Grab your coats girls and let's go."

Juan ran up to the back door, "Mr. Sam we're ready to ride."

"Sally Jo wants you to hook up the buckboard. She wants to go too in case Rosa needs her."

"Right,"

"Okay Sally Jo, grab a shawl. Juan leave one of the boys to drive the buckboard, the rest of you get in the saddle."

Billy Joe didn't say a word, he just reached down and unbuckled his gun belt and looped it around the saddle horn. Slipped his feet out of the stirrups and threw his left leg over the horses head and flew off the back of his horse. Hitting the ground right in front of the belligerent private. The same instant his boots hit the ground, the knuckles on his rock hard right fist slammed into the point of the private's chin. Snapping his head back like he had been hit with a bois-d'arc post.

The man's feet flew up and he sat down hard on his back pockets. He shook his head, bewildered to find himself in that position in front of all his new found friends, then he bellowed like a raging bull and leaped to his feet. He came in swinging those big ponderous fists like he was fighting off a swarm of bees. One of the blows caught Billy Joe square on the jaw and knocked him to the ground.

As soon as Billy Joe was on the ground the big private tried to kick him with those hobnailed army boots. Just as the man drew back his right foot to kick, Billy Joe flipped around and jammed the heel of his cowboy boot into the man's left knee. His leg buckled and he hit the ground beside Billy Joe.

Billy Joe was the first back to his feet and when the big brute tried to jump up Billy Joe let fly. His right fist crashed into the private's nose like a freight train hitting a buffalo. The big dude sprawled out in the dirt, but the old private was game. He rolled over and was charging back before you could blink an eye.

He landed a heavy blow right above Billy Joe's right eye and blood started to cloud his vision in that eye. They went toe to toe for several seconds. The crowd was growing and loving the action. Some were even making bets on the winner.

All at once Billy Joe dropped under the man's blows and rammed his forehead against the man's chest and started hammering him in the bread basket. After about three hard blows to the stomach all of that alcohol he had consumed came up. He was doubled over puking up his toe nails. All the fight was gone out of him, he was too busy retching. Then more fights broke out around the ring when people tried to collect on bets.

Billy Joe looked up and saw six solders wielding batons marching toward the fray.

⊫≕⊹ ⊹≕⊐

Sally Jo sat on the bouncing buckboard and prayed, **Lord I don't know what kind of accident we are gonna find when we get there. I know you can go on ahead of us and make sure that they are alright. We know somebody is hurt because they said they need the doctor. Lord if it's Mr. C or Rosa or Russ, we ask your special care for them, Lord it don't matter which one of them is hurt, please help 'em. Lord give us the wisdom to do the right thing, so we don't make the matter worse by doing the wrong thing. Lord, Russ and Rosa are supposed to get married in two weeks don't**

let this keep them from getting married. Please help us Lord. In your precious son's name I'm asking.

⟞⟝ ⟞⟝

Huge clods of dirt flew up behind the racing horses as the men from the W-H made a mad dash across the plains toward the Tumbling C. Even though they were moving at a break neck speed Sam was able to get from the rider, now mounted on a new horse, that one of the drill stems broke and knocked one of the legs on the derrick drill tower loose and the whole tower collapsed on the men.

As they topped a ridge they could see below a devastating scene. All that was left of the giant drilling rig was a pile of large sticks piled haphazardly in a heap. Worse yet Sam immediately saw oil seeping up out of the hole and spreading among the collapsed timbers.

"Whatever you men do, do-not strike a match, this whole place will go up in flames. We've gotta move fast, it's gonna be dark pretty soon."

"Where is Mr. C?"

The man who had come for help just pointed at the pile of debris.

"Men, be careful don't climb up on the pile because your weight might crush somebody pinned underneath. Start working from the outside in, work in pairs. Two men on a piece of timber. Careful not to make a spark, look at all that oil seeping in among the debris. All it will take is one spark and we'll have an inferno."

Working as quickly and as safely as they could one by one they removed the large pieces of timber that had been used to erect the drilling derrick. It was a race against the setting sun, as darkness slowly settled over the crash site. Painstakingly slow they found men buried under the pile of broken timbers.

"Sam, we have got to have light. It is too dark to see what we're doing."

Pointing at two of the men Sam said, "You two race back to the Tumbling *C* and get two lanterns."

"Sam what about the fire hazard?"

"We still have not found Joe Carville. We can't stop until they are all out from under that pile of lumber."

"But Sam, if a fire starts that will be a funeral pyre."

"I know, but I have an idea that might work. If this pile explodes, we can all be dead. While we're waiting I'm going to say a prayer. If any of you have any connections with the man up above now would be a good time for you to be contacting him too."

CHAPTER TWELVE

Billy Joe pulled off to the east end of the line of people and after taking care of his horses spread his bed roll. When he tried to lay down he found a few sore spots that he hadn't had yesterday. "I'll say this much that big private could throw a punch that's for sure."

At first light Billy Joe was up, washed his face in the cold river water and led his horses down to drink. Some dude had set up a grill on a pile of rocks and was selling flapjacks for a quarter apiece. Billy Joe wandered over there to see what was happening. He saw a homemade sign that read flapjacks two bits, bring your own plate. When he looked the man had gallon buckets of maple syrup sitting on the tail gate of his wagon and his wife was selling the flapjacks as fast as he could turn them off the grill.

Billy Joe walked up and handed the lady two quarters and said, "I'll take two."

She said, "Hand me your plate and fill your cup with coffee."

As Billy Joe was squatting to one side eating his flapjack a shadow fell over him. He looked up and the old private was standing over him. He started to set his plate down on the ground when the man stuck out his big hand and said, "Put 'er there mic, I'll shake your hand, I'll say this you ain't real big but sure pack a good whollop."

Billy Joe got to his feet and reached up and rubbed his jaw, "I'll say this you sure did make eating these flapjacks a lot harder yourself." and shook the man's hand.

"If anybody gives you any trouble you tell them you are a friend of Timothy O'Leary. You just send for me and I will come." He turned and walked away.

The cannon to start the race was scheduled to go off at straight up noon. About two hours before the race was to start people were already jostling each other for a place to start from.

Billy Joe eased his two horses into the line between two wagons. He felt safer here than out there with all those milling horses and mules. He could hear cussing and yelling all up and down the line. A big Swede was driving the wagon on his left and a big black man with a wagon load of grown boys riding in it on the right, so Billy Joe figured this was the safest place he could be, nobody was going to move either one of those wagons.

The army had sharp shooters with rifles standing every fifty feet apart facing the river on the Oklahoma side. Billy Joe kept craning his neck up and down the line looking for Mary Beth and her father.

The big Swede said, "You be looking for somebody?"

"Yeah, I met a man with a pretty dark haired daughter the other day but I haven't been able to find them since I got back from scouting the land."

The big Swede grinned and said, "I think it is not the man you look for."

Billy Joe felt his ears turning red and said, "Sir you are correct. I sure would like to see that young lady again."

"Well my friend it is a big country and we are going to be here a long time. If it is meant to be you will find her again, I'm thinking."

Being between the two wagons did keep him out of the hustle and bustle but it also kept any breeze from getting to him. As the sun moved higher in the sky it got hotter and his own horses started to fidget. The crescendo of cussing grew louder, men cussing each other, men cussing stubborn mules, men cussing frisky horses, it was a lot of noise.

One man eased his horse down into the river and a soldier fired a shot into the water in front of him and he jerked his horse back to the bank.

Billy Joe watched the shadow cast by the wagon on his right slowly back up to the east. He knew when that shadow was directly under the wagon it would be time to go.

Billy Joe thought he heard the cannon, he wasn't really sure all he knew was those two wagons started to move so he raked his spurs along the flank of his horse and leaped into the water as one hundred thousand other horses churned the red river into a soup of water and red clay. He had a fleeting thought that those soldiers were going to get trampled. Then he was off and running. Driving straight for the survey flag he had chosen.

He had a good horse and he could run. Any thought of Christian civility seemed to be completely forgotten by most of the people in this race, he saw men knocked from horses, and he saw wagons upset, spilling people and goods on the ground. One time he was racing neck and neck with another horse when the horse stumbled and threw the rider over the horses head and other horses behind them ran right over the man. Billy Joe had seen cattle stampede, and this looked like a stampede. His only hope for survival was to stay out in front of the herd of horses and mules charging across the prairie at break neck speed.

After a couple of miles the herd started to thin out as people swung off in different directions and people stopped to claim a survey flag they had chosen. He was able to slow the horses to a fast trot before he killed the animals. Soon he looked around and he was riding alone at the moment so he slowed the horses to a walk, but he did not stop. He kept moving steadily toward the mountain he could see in the distance.

All at once he looked up and saw a cloud of dust coming toward him from the north. Then it occurred to him, they had two starting lines, one north and one south. So he kicked his horse back up to full speed. He had not thought that people would be coming from the north also. After a few minutes, he could see the pass in the hills he was aiming for. Then he could see a paint horse coming at a full gallop from the north and it appeared to be headed for the same gap.

He lost sight of the paint horse as his horses raced down into a gulley. When they topped out on the other side he looked and he had about another mile to go but the paint horse appeared to be even closer.

Billy Joe urged B.J. to try harder. He knew B.J. was getting tired but he had heart and everything was riding on them getting to that survey flag first. Then the other horse went into a low place and Billy Joe lost sight of it. Now he was laying on B.J.'s neck to cut down on the wind resistance. He took a chance and turned loose of the lead rope, hoping the packhorse would follow them. It had better because all his supplies were on that horse but if that paint horse got to the flag first it wouldn't matter where his supplies were.

Half a mile, just a half mile then he spotted the other horse as it rose up on level ground again, it was no more than a half mile from the flag. "Come on B.J., I know you 're tuckered but you gotta do it, you can do it, give it all you've got."

Looking again they were down to a quarter of a mile and the other rider was beating his horse with a quirt. Billy Joe thought '*I would never do that to BJ, never.*

CHAPTER THIRTEEN

Sally Jo said, "Rosa we can't help them, all we can do is pray for the men who are hurt and the men who are trying to help them."

"I don't even know who's hurt and how bad." Rosa said.

"I don't know either. All I know is somebody out there is still giving orders because somebody sent a rider to our place to get help."

"Oh, Sally Jo I can't stand it if it's Russ. We are supposed to get married next Saturday." She broke down and sobbed.

Sally Jo hugged her friend and said, "We need to pray."

Rosa wiped her eyes on the hem of her apron and said, "I can't stand it if it's Mr. C, any more than if it's Russ."

"Caroline why don't you and Mattie get some coffee brewing because they are gonna need it when they do get through."

Sally Jo opened up Rosa's Bible that was lying on the table beside the fire place and it opened to Psalms 46:1

God is our refuge and strength, an ever-present help in trouble. Therefore we will not fear...

Rosa listen to this, "God is our refuge and strength, an ever-present help in trouble. Therefore, we will not fear."

"Oh, Lord God we confess we do feel terrified right now. We lift our fears up to you. Merciful Father, keep all who are working to rescue and bring relief all who might be injured this night here at this ranch. Give them courage in danger, skill in difficulty, and compassion in service. Sustain them with bodily strength and calmness of mind that they may perform the job to the well-being of those in need so that lives may be saved.

Father we pray for your compassion and protection on those who need rescuing and the men who are laboring to save them.

In Jesus name, Amen."

Sally Jo said, "Why don't we make a big pot of coffee and take it out to the well site. The guys will need some coffee soon."

Rosa wiped her eyes again and said, "I have a dish pan full of donuts, the guys always like their bear signs."

Caroline said, "Billy Joe will probably smell them all the way up in Oklahoma and come racing back. You know how that boy loves your bear signs."

Rosa smiled then and said, "I'd make 'em every day if it would get that boy back home."

"Yes, Rosa I would too. I pray for that boy every night. Oh I know he's a man. But he'll always be our little boy."

"Sally Jo do you remember when that rattlesnake almost got him and God sent a chaparral to kill the snake."

Mattie said, "What are you talking about?"

"Rosa and I were out picking beans in the garden. Billy Joe was a little tyke about two years old. He wandered off a little ways and Rosa happened to look up as Billy Joe was reaching to get a bean off the vine and a big diamond back rattler was coiled ready to strike Billy Joe. We both screamed but before either one of us could do anything a big Road Runner zipped out from between the plants and killed that snake before it could strike Billy Joe."

"I didn't know a Road Runner could kill a Rattlesnake?""

"I didn't either until that one did it. Grandpa says they do it all the time. The only natural predator to a Rattlesnake is a Road Runner."

"All this time I thought they just look cute running down the road." Caroline said.

"Okay, ladies, let's take a big urn of coffee and a batch of Rosa's donuts and go out to the well site and see what's going on."

As the buckboard drew closer to the well site the four ladies were shocked when they saw what was going on. Two men stood in their stirrups about fifty feet out from the pile of timbers that had once been an oil well, each one holding a lantern high over his head. Everybody else was pulling large pieces of timber one piece at a time and carrying it over to the side and piling it on the growing pile. Then race back for another piece, then all at once they lifted a man out of the rubble and hurried over to a wagon parked about one hundred feet away. The doctor was working in the wagon.

Sally Jo said, "There's Russ. He's one of the ones carrying others to the wagon where the doctor is."

"Oh, thank you Jesus." Rosa said.

"I don't see Sam?"

"I don't either but I hear him. He's the one telling everybody what to do." Caroline said.

Everything was quiet for a minute then Mattie said, "Where's grandpa?"

Soon they were down to a hundred yards, Billy Joe thought 'the paint horse is starting to fade.

B.J. expanded his ribcage, got a second wind and tore across the last fifty yards. Billy Joe guided B.J. so the flag would pass by on his left side. He leaned over like a polo player and snatched the flag out of the ground with his left hand and snatched his six-shooter out with his right hand. When he slowed B.J. and turned around the other horse was down on his knees and the rider was pulling a six-shooter out of his holster. Billy Joe cocked back the hammer on his six-shooter and said, "Hold it mister. I don't know whether you plan to shoot that horse or me but you're not going to shoot either one. Now drop it back in your holster real easy and get your hand away from it or I'll drill you right where you stand."

He could see the man was fighting mad but he was no fool, he could see the business end of Billy Joe's forty-four was lined up on his chest.

The man glared at Billy Joe but he dropped the gun back in the holster.

"Mister I hope you had a second choice in mind because this one's mine. I won the race. Now ease that horse back up on his feet and lead him on to your second choice. Too bad you ran him so hard he may never be the same. In fact here is what I'll do. I'll swap you my pack horse for that one and ten dollars."

"I don't want your horse."

"Then you better start walking 'cause all the survey flags may already be gone. But if they are not they sure will be pretty soon."

The guy looked around and he could see riders spreading out all across the range. He reached in his jeans and pulled out a ten dollar gold piece, "Here. Take that pack saddle off so I can put my saddle on."

Billy Joe stepped down, careful to keep the pack horse between him and the other man. He pulled the pack saddle off the horse.

He stepped back and watched the man strap on his saddle. Billy Joe didn't move or put the thong back on his six-shooter until the man rode off. Then he went to the paint horse and gently encouraged the horse back to his feet. Led it slowly to a creek near by and let it drink a little water. "That's enough for now. I'll give you some more in a few minutes."

He worked with the horse for an hour, slowly he would lead it around in a big circle then bring it back for some more water. Little by little the animal responded until after an hour or so it had settled down. Then Billy Joe staked both horses on some good grass and proceeded to set up his camp. Several times he heard shooting off in the distance. No one had come close to his camp yet.

That night Billy Joe sat alone near his camp fire and listened to the night sounds. Every place has its own night sounds once your mind gets used to them then you will know in an instant if something strange happens.

It was a beautiful night, the moon was full, bathing the entire area in a soft glow, the quail calling from the grass, the mournful sound of the turtle dove in the brush, a hoot owl high up on the mountain querying the night. On the other side of the pass a coyote was serenading the moon. His horses quietly cropping grass near the camp fire. Billy Joe felt good, this was his land, and it would become whatever he made of it. It was a start, to following his dream.

According to the printed paper they gave him, someone would be around in a few days to record his name and issue a deed for this piece of land to him. Early the next morning he was up at first light. The first thing he did was see to the horses. B.J. was fine, the paint still looked a little peaked but he seemed to be doing fine he just needed a few days rest. That fool pushed this horse way too fast too far.

He had decided that he would build a house on the shelf facing south with the mountain up behind him. That way the house would be protected from the cold north wind by the mountain.

He grabbed an ax and started felling trees, clearing a spot for the house. The work was hard and by mid-morning he was wet with sweat but it felt good. Late that afternoon he had felled and cleaned the limbs off twenty tall trees, when a couple of men in a large wagon approached his camp. Billy Joe had his six-shooter on, he reached down and slipped the thong off the hammer, eased over to where he had hung his shirt on a branch and slipped it on then casually picked up his Winchester. "Howdy."

"Howdy, we're gonna be your neighbors, we've got the next survey out there on the flat. We're wondering if you'd sell us them logs you've cut so we can start putting up a house. Don't care much for them sod houses."

They dickered around and settled on ten dollars a log, using his horses as a team they managed to load ten of the logs on the wagon and the men paid him one hundred dollars. "We'll be back in the morning for the rest of 'em if we need more can we come back?"

"Yes sir. Pleasure doing business with ya."

"You never did tell us your name."

"I guess we got so busy loading logs we never introduced ourselves, my name is Billy Joe McClanton."

"I'm Jeffrey Thomas, all my friends just call me Jeff and this is my brother- in-law. His name is Chester Wilson, most people just call him Chet."

After they drove away Billy Joe set about fixing some supper. He was thinking, *I made two hundred dollars today. That ain't a bad start. You know instead of selling them a whole tree for ten dollars if I had one of them saw mills I could cut them trees up into boards and get a lot more than ten dollars a tree.*

That night as Billy Joe sat by his fire he was still brooding about losing the Bible and breaking his promise to his mother. When out of the night he heard a voice say "Hello the camp. May I come in?"

The voice sounded like an old man, Billy Joe took the thong off his six-gun then said, "Come on in."

A really old emancipated Indian walked up to the fire. He looked like he hadn't eaten in several days. Billy Joe said, "I have beans and bacon. Here is a plate, help yourself."

"Thank you my friend, Chippewa Joe not had food in many moons."

"That's your name, Chippewa Joe?"

"That is what white man call me."

"Okay Chippewa. Where is your horse?"

"No have horse, walk."

"Chippewa my name is Billy Joe McClanton. You're welcome to eat with me any time you want."

"You good man Billy Joe McClanton. Chippewa saw what you do for paint horse."

"Oh, it was nothing; in fact, he's okay now. He turned out to be a good horse and I got, ten dollars to boot. So, it was a good deal for me,"

"Billy Joe McClanton, Chippewa Joe has a book he cannot read. You take you read." He reached into a pack on his back and pulled out a Bible and handed it to Billy Joe.

Billy Joe stared at it. It was a Bible just like the one his mother had given him. He lifted the cover and stared at his name written in his mother's hand writing. He stared in total disbelief, then turned to say something to the old Indian and he was not there, he had walked off into the night.

Billy Joe was bewildered, he held on to the Bible tightly, and then he noticed a tree leaf stuck in between the pages. He opened the Bible to the page where the tree leaf was and read:

Be not forgetful to entertain strangers: for thereby some have entertained angels unawares.

Looking at the verse it was Hebrews 13:2.

CHAPTER FOURTEEN

Every man was out and being seen to except Joe Carville. The amount of oil coming out of the hole was increasing. At first it was seeping now it was flowing. After removing a dozen more broken and tangled timbers one of the men said "I can see him. He is right at the edge of the plat-form. The oil is running right down on his legs and feet."

One of the other men said, "Boy that oil coming up out of the ground is hot."

"Four of you guys grab the end of those timbers and lift them as high as you can, I'm going in there to get Joe."

Russ said, "Wait Sam, this stack is getting ready to blow. Joe may already be dead. We can't afford to lose you too."

"Push and pray guys, I've got to go get 'im." When Sam dropped down on his belly and started to crawl under the pile, suddenly it was so dark under the stack he could barely make out the light-colored shirt Joe Carville was wearing. Sliding on his belly like a snake he started to work his way under the pile, it looked like he had about twenty feet to go to get to Joe.

Russ yelled, "We need some more help over here. These timbers are too heavy. We can't hold 'em up. Sam will be crushed if we drop this pile."

Sam realized he was crawling through a solid mass of oil, it was getting hotter under there. He thought if we get a spark, me and Joe are gonna be fried to a crisp. He still had fifteen more feet to go to reach Joe. Suddenly he felt a sharp pain in the back of his right shoulder. The timber had sagged down and a sharp nail had stabbed into the back of his shoulder. He couldn't move. "Russ, you've got to lift it up higher I'm stuck."

Russ glanced over his left shoulder and saw the buckboard Sally Jo and Rosa came in. "One of you boys unhook that horse from the buck board and back it under the end of these timbers we'll jam it under here and take some of the strain off of us. Okay guys on three heave these timbers up higher, one, two, three, heave." The timbers groaned as the men lifted several hundred pounds of twisted and broken wood and metal. ***Oh God don't let any metal scrape and cause a spark.***

Four big strong men's muscles strained and sweat poured down their bodies. Two of the other men pushed the buckboard backward under the end of the timber the men were lifting. "Okay men give it one more push get it under a little more."

Sam felt the release when the nail was lifted out of his shoulder he estimated he still had ten more feet before he could reach Joe.

Sally Jo and Rosa set the coffee and donuts on the tail gate of the tool wagon and watched in horror to the drama unfolding in front of them. They could hear what was going on, Caroline said, "Mama is daddy going under there to get grandpa?"

Mattie started to cry. Rosa hugged her and said, "Honey, all we can do is pray." The four women felt so helpless as they stood and watched.

Sam was finally able to get a hand on Joe's left arm. When he tried to pull him he realized Joe was so covered in oil he couldn't get a grip, his hand kept sliding off. He felt panic, then he reached down and jerked off his belt and buckled it around Joe's wrist and his hands were so covered in oil he couldn't hold on to the belt, his hand kept slipping off. Desperately he tried several times then he did the only thing he could think of he put the end of the belt in his mouth and bit down hard with his teeth. Then slowly he started to squirm backward dragging the dead weight of Joe Carville with him. Ever so slowly he squirmed back hoping the pile held until he could get them out.

Sam felt hands grabbing his ankles and someone was pulling him, he still gripped the end of his belt in his teeth, even though his jaws were aching.

Russ said, "Let go of the belt Sam we've got 'im." Then Russ helped Sam who was coated in oil from his head to his feet. "Sally Jo and the girls are over there by the tool wagon. Go let them see you are alright even if you are covered in oil and stink to high heaven. I'll still bet they'll be glad to see you, I know I am. We'll get Joe over to the doc and let him check 'im over."

Sally Jo picked up a feed sack lying on the floor of the tool wagon and handed it to Sam. "I would hug you, you fool husband of mine, but not with all that oil all over you. That was the bravest thing I've ever seen you do."

Rosa asked, "Sam, Mr. C., alright?"

Sam slipped his shirt off as he wiped oil off his face and arms. "I don't know. It was so dark under there I couldn't tell. I just knew I had to get him out of there."

As Sam continued to wipe the oil off suddenly Sally Jo said, "Sam you need to go let the doctor look at you. Your back is covered in blood."

CHAPTER FIFTEEN

S am had just walked over to the wagon where the doctor was treating Joe. "What do you think doc? Is he going to be alright?"

"I tell you the truth. I don't know. He took a hit to the head, and he has a broken shoulder. I wouldn't be surprised if he hasn't cracked a few ribs. I have no way of knowing about internal damage. I'm getting ready to take him back to my house so I can keep an eye on him for a few days." Then he spotted the blood on Sam's back. "Here let me look at you."

He applied a poultice to Sam's shoulder and wrapped it up. Just as he finished there was a loud whoosh. The entire rig burst into fire. The flames shot a hundred feet in the air. All at once it was light as noon day.

Sam was running fast to Sally Jo and the girls, "Move this thing way back it may get a lot worse."

The wind was picking up caused by the intense heat of the well fire. The grass and brush on the west side of the well burst into flames. "Russ get some men over there and stop that prairie fire, we can't let this thing spread."

The fire was making a loud roaring sound as it shot straight up out of the hole like a torch. Oil was burning all around the well.

One of the experienced drillers ran up and said the only way to put out a well fire is to blow it out with dynamite and there was some in the tool wagon. Sam looked over and his heart almost stopped, Sally Jo and his girls were standing beside that tool wagon.

"Go move that tool wagon farther away from here and tell my wife not to stand near it. Then bring me some sticks of dynamite, let's see what we can do."

The men on the downwind side were fighting a valiant fight to keep the fire from spreading. It was obvious they were not going to be able to contain it unless they could get the main source put out.

The driller ran back up with an arm full of dynamite sticks. Sam grabbed one of the sticks and pulled a match out of his pocket, "Stand back. We don't know what is gonna happen when we set this thing off."

Sam struck the match and touched it to the fuse on the dynamite stick. It started to fiz and sparkle, gritting his teeth against the pain in his right shoulder he threw it as far into the burning mass as he could. The explosion was much larger than he expected. Large burning timbers flew up in the air like match sticks. Miraculously the fire around the blowing hole in the ground was blowing out.

Then as he watched, it reignited from the burning well. Then it spread right back out where it was. The heat was so intense he could not get any closer. Maybe one of the other men could throw it closer to the well than he could with this bum shoulder.

"I need someone who can throw better than I can."

"Let me have it," Russ said.

Sam looked at Russ and said, "No Russ, let one of the others. If Joe doesn't make it and something happens to me. Rosa and Sally Jo will need you. One of us needs to step back for them."

Without hesitating Russ said, "You're right. You step back and let me take this."

"Russ, I can't. Send me someone."

Over the next hour the heat and pressure kept building as several men tried. They could blow out the fire around the well and quickly the intense fire from the well would reignite it.

Sam looked up and neighbors, attracted to the roaring flame lighting the night sky, gathered to watch what was happening. He thought *people please stay back we don't have any idea what this thing is gonna do next, the whole earth may explode in a little while if the fire goes underground.'*

One of the drillers stepped up beside Sam and said, "I 've got a large wooden plug to drive down into the drill pipe as soon as you blow it out, if you can figure out a way to blow it out, otherwise it will just reignite as soon as fresh oil shoots out and hits a spark."

"We have got to get that dynamite to the well hole and blow that out. We can stop the rest as soon as that monster is killed."

All at once an old Indian appeared to walk up to the fire. "I watch white brother throw stick into fire and boom fire gone, except never into center of fire. Must get boom stick to center of fire."

"Old timer you are right. Do you know how to put boom stick in middle of fire?"

"Tie your boom stick to arrow and Chippewa Joe shoot it into fire."

Sam stared at him then he noticed the old Indian held a bow in his right hand and had a quiver of arrows on his back. "Do you think you can do it?"

"Chippewa Joe know how to shoot arrow since a papoose."

"Find some twine. We have tried everything else." One of the guys ran back with a ball of twine. Sam said. "Okay before we try this we need to make sure we have a plan in case it works."

The driller spoke up, "As soon as the fire poofs out two of us will race to the well. I'll jam this wooden plug into the pipe and Wilson here will use that sledge hammer to drive it down. We'll hope it doesn't blow back out."

"What if it does blow back out?"

"Me and Wilson will hope we can run fast enough to get out of there before it reignites."

Sam looked up at the night sky and said, "Lord I hope you can hear me over the roar of this fire. We need your help."

The old Indian said, "He heard."

They tied the unlit stick of dynamite to the arrow and Chippewa Joe pulled the bow back until the bow string was taught. Then Sam touched a match to the fuse on the dynamite.

The old Indian held the bow steady so long Sam was starting to think, 'Let it go man. Don't let that thing go off right here. Why doesn't he let it go?'

All at once the arrow arched high in the sky. streams of sparks flying from it, then it arched down into the center of the inferno.

There was a loud boom, the ground latterly shook and the fire blew out. It was suddenly pitch dark. Sam heard feet running beside him, then he heard a loud thump as a big hammer drove a wedge down in the drill pipe.

He looked around to thank the Indian but he was no longer there.

CHAPTER SIXTEEN

Billy Joe was fixing breakfast when three hard cases rode up. One of them said, "Snake, I think this gent has enough breakfast for all of us."

The three sat their horses looking all around his camp. "I see he still has the survey flag. That means they haven't come around and recorded who got here first. Maybe this is a good place. I see somebody has cleared a place for us to build a nice house right over there."

Billy Joe was squatted on his heels and knew he had no chance to stand up and take the thong of his six-shooter before they filled him full of lead. He said, "Dismount friends, I've got plenty of coffee, biscuits and bacon."

He had already slipped on his work gloves so he could handle the hot skillet handle. He sat the pan down and sliced off several more slices of salt pork into the skillet. "Bring your own cup and plate I'm a little short of dishes right now."

The three, ground hitched their horses and pulled a tin cup and tin plate out of their saddle bags. They sat down cross legged on the opposite side of the fire from Billy Joe. The one they called Snake looked at Billy Joe and said, "Ain't I seen you someplace before?"

"I don't think so. Where you from?"

"Texas."

"Texas is a big place. Where bouts in Texas."

Billy Joe knew he was in trouble. He needed to be careful. "Yeah, it is. What about you gents, where you hail from?"

"You ever been to a town called Cactus Tree?" Snake asked.

"I've probably passed through there. Is that where you boys are from?"

Two of the ruffians were sopping their biscuit in the bacon grease. Snake's eyes narrowed, "Is your pa Sam McClanton?"

The other two stopped eating and stared at Billy Joe.

"Do you know Sam McClanton?"

"Yeah, I know him I still got marks on my back from his whip. I think you're his kid. As soon as I finish eatin' this bacon I'm gonna kill ya. I'm gonna do it slow and every blow will be one for your old man."

Billy Joe thought, *everybody you entertain sure ain't no angel.* He poured himself another cup of coffee and when he reached to set the coffee pot back on the coals his gloved right hand slid down the side of the pot and scooped up a hand full of glowing coals of fire and threw them straight into Snake's face. Snake screamed and fell over backward.

In one swift fluid motion Billy Joe was on his feet with a six-shooter in his right hand. The man on the far left had risen half-way to his feet and was pulling out a six-shooter when a forty-four slug made the third button on his shirt disappear.

Snake was rolling around on the ground moaning, his hands over his face. Billy Joe aimed the forty-four straight at the other man and said, "I can bury one or three it don't matter none to me. You've got one minute to get your two buddies off my land. I know what you look like and if I ever see you again you better have a gun in your hand, 'cause, I'm gonna come shootin'. Now unless you want me to dump all three of you in one grave you better get off my land. I sure ain't gonna waste my time digging three holes for buzzard meat like you three. I don't know why my pa took a whip to big mouth there, if I did I'd probably put a bullet in you two right now. Move it."

As the one hombre rode away leading the other two horses Billy Joe sat back down and poured himself another cup of coffee. Thinking *grandpa has got a steam powered saw out behind his barn that he used to cut the lumber to build his buildings. I'll bet he would loan it to me and then if I could get it moved up here I could set it up and sell boards to the other settlers. I can't leave here until they come and record my name on this deed, somebody else will come and claim it if I leave now.*

All day long he felled every fifth tree so he wouldn't strip all the trees off the land. He knew if he did water would wash off all the top soil and no trees would grow back. "Whoa," Billy Joe had hooked the two horses up to drag the felled trees down to the area where he planned to set up the saw mill. When two men in army uniforms rode up.

"Do you have the survey flag?"

"Yes sir I do, it's right here."

"As the sergeant recorded Billy Joe's name and survey number the other man looked around and said, "It looks like you are already working. What are you planning to build with all those logs?"

"Actually I felled twenty trees to build a house in that clearing but before I could get started a couple of men came over and bought the logs from me. So I got to thinking if they would buy logs they would probably buy boards and I could get more out of each tree. So I'm gonna go get me a saw mill and start cutting boards for folks who want to build a house or barn."

"Son, I think that is a great idea. Do you know where you can get a saw mill?"

"Yes sir, my grandpa has got one out behind his barn and I'm gonna go borrow it or buy it from him."

The Sergeant said, "Son watch out for three hard cases that are slipping around out here causing trouble. We haven't been able to catch 'em yet. They killed a family man about ten miles west of here and molested his wife."

"Sir there ain't but two of 'em now."

"Why do you say that?"

Billy Joe told him what had happened when the three had stopped by his place.

"Well son you did good. I just wish you had shot all three of 'em. Snake's the leader, he's the worst one of the bunch. You say he got glowing hot coals in his face. Be interesting to see if it left scars."

⊨⊣⊢⊨

Ten days later Juan looked up and said, "You late. Work started many hours now."

Billy Joe jumped off of B.J. and hugged his old friend. "Good to see you too, you old outlaw."

"Your mama, she look to the north every day, looking for el niño."

"Juan, you forgot I grew up with you, I know niño, means little boy, do I look like poquito niño to you?"

Billy Joe stepped in the back door, Sally Jo heard the door open and turned. She ran over and had to reach up to hug her son. "Why are you back so soon? Are you alright? You aren't sick, are you?"

Laughing he said, "No Mother. I'm not sick so don't even think about getting that Castor oil out."

He told her about his idea of setting up a saw mill. "I remembered grandpa has that old stream mill out behind the barn. I'm going to see if he'll sell it to me or loan it to me."

Her eyes took on a sad expression and she said, "You don't know about the accident."

Billy Joe was reaching for a cold biscuit and stopped in mid stride, "What accident?"

She told him about the accident at the drilling rig. "Billy Joe, I 've never been so scared in my life. Your grandpa was trapped under that heap of timber and oil was spreading over everything. Your father crawled under that pile of debris and rescued your grandpa. I was terrified that the whole thing was going to catch on fire and both of them would be killed. It was horrible to see. I had nightmares for several nights."

"Is pa alright?'

"Yes. He only had a nail puncture in the back of his shoulder. He's fine."

"How is grandpa?"

"Not so good, he was hurt pretty bad. He had several broken bones, the worst thing is he had a head injury. We just brought him home from the doctor's clinic yesterday. Rosa's taking care of him. You can run over there and see him after supper. He'll be tickled to see you."

CHAPTER SEVENTEEN

When Billy Joe walked into his grandpa's house, Rosa threw down her dish towel and ran over to the door and hugged him. "Oh, my goodness it's good to see you. Your grandpa's going to be so surprised. Let me look at you."

"Good to see you too Rosa. How is grandpa?"

"Billy Joe, I better warn you. He's hurt but we're going to help him get better." Then she smiled and said, "But the best medicine will be when he sees you."

When Billy Joe walked into his grandfather's room, he was not prepared for what he saw. The person laying propped up in the bed was not the stalwart bigger than life man he had always looked up to. Instead was a shriveled up white haired man with skin that looked translucent.

"Oh my goodness Billy Joe, come over here and let me look at you. Sorry I am a little stove up right now, so I can't jump up and hug your neck. Rosa won't let me get up yet."

"Yeah, grandpa I know how tough Rosa can be." *He looks bad but his voice sounds the same.*

"I'll make you think bad, if I catch you trying to sneak your hand in my cookie jar while you're here." She said.

"Rosa, do we have any coffee left. I think I could use a cup. What about you Billy Joe?"

"Yeah, if Rosa has any made, I'll go get us a cup."

"No, you won't. You sit down there and talk to the grouchy old man and I'll get you both some coffee."

"How are things going? Have you gotten some land?"

For the next several minutes Billy Joe told him about the land he had gotten the deed to. He failed to mention any fights or shooting. "I felled twenty logs to start a house but before I could get them laid out two men came and paid me ten dollars apiece for them. So I got to thinking. I chose this land because of the valley on the other side of the pass, but the business may be cutting lumber for all those other folks who got land out there to use for building. So, I remembered that old saw mill you've got out behind the barn. I wonder if you would be willing to sell it or loan it to me so I can start sawing lumber. I've got lots of tall trees."

"That's a smart move Billy Joe. I won't loan it to you I'll give it to you. You'll need to get you a tractor to run it though."

"No sir, I want to use the old steam engine. Gasoline is gonna be hard to come by up there in the territory but I've got plenty of firewood and a good spring for water."

"I see what cha mean. You'll have to figure out how to get it up there to your place. Russ can help you. I wish I could go with you."

"Grandpa, you just mind Rosa and pretty soon maybe you and pa can come up there and see what I've got going on."

Two weeks later a large wagon pulled by six big mules with a sawmill on it rumbled into the area where Billy Joe wanted to set it up. A smaller wagon pulled by a team of mules followed with a boiler for the steam pot. It took a week of hard work before they heard the whine of the giant saw blade as the first logs were sent down to the mill.

Billy Joe hired four of the homesteaders who already had their crop planted to help run the sawmill. They agreed to take cut lumber for their pay so they would have material for their own building needs. Two of the guys were felling trees while the other two were busy cutting and stacking ten foot lengths of boards.

"Guys y'all keep cutting and stacking. I'm gonna get on my horse and ride around telling the other neighbors that we've got sawed lumber for sale. I'll be back before dark."

CHAPTER EIGHTEEN

The doctor unwound the bandage off Snakes face. "The burns look like they're healing pretty good. You're gonna have some scars that won't go away."

Snake gingerly felt of his face and snarled, "I'm gonna kill that jasper."

Leroy said, "Snake, I say we ride north and see what we can find up there. The daddy whopped you with a whip. Now the boy done burned you in the face. It's like playing poker sometimes you just gotta know when to move on to another game. Just like his daddy, he done told us what he was gonna do if he ever saw either one of us again and I believe him. I say we ride up in the north part where he ain't and hope there ain't no more of them."

"I'm gonna kill him and then go back and kill his pa. That's what I'm gonna do. The old man thinks he can whoop me like a mule and then the kid burned my face and left me lookin' like a freak. I'm gonna kill all of 'em."

"Right now, let's ride up in the north part of the territory and we'll figure out a plan."

"I tell you, I'm gonna kill ever one of 'em."

Everywhere they looked construction was going on. Soon there would be a real town here on the prairie. As they walked down the street they met a young cowhand who stared at Snake.

"What are you lookin' at?"

"No offence mister, I was just wondering how you got burnt?"

"I'll make you stare at me like I'm a freak."

Snake whipped out his six-shooter and put two forty-four slugs in the young man's chest.

The blacksmith yelled, "Hey what are you doin'? He said he was sorry."

Snake shot him.

A crowd of armed men were running in their direction to see what was going on. Snake and Leroy jumped on their horses and raced north out of town.

CHAPTER NINETEEN

A strong gust of wind caught the top of the tree just as the ax bit through the last of the strands of wood holding the tree straight up, causing the tree to fall back the wrong way. The young farmer that Billy Joe had hired to help fell trees tried to jump out of the way of the falling tree. He almost made it. Two thousand pounds of hard wood crashed down on him.

The whine of the big steel wood cutting blade filled the air, no other sound could be heard.

The young man driving the team skidding the logs down to the saw mill came back leading the team of mules. At first he was confused. He expected to see more logs ready to transport to the sawmill. He could only see one downed tree and it wasn't ready to move, the limbs hadn't been trimmed off. He looked around for Lester, where was he and why had he not cut any more logs?

What's that under the tree? Pulling apart some of the leaves he saw a checkered shirt under the brush. Frantically he pulled the branches apart until he could see the back of Lester's checkered shirt. Lester was pinned under the felled tree. He was face down in the dirt, so he couldn't tell if he was still breathing or not.

Running down the hill as fast as his boots could move, he yelled at the top of his voice but the whine of the sawblade made hearing him impossible. Grabbing the saw mill operator on the shoulder he shouted, "Shut it down. I need your help, a tree fell on Lester."

"I can't until this log gets to the end. Hold on." As soon as the twenty foot log reached the end of the shuttle the operator raced over and opened the steam release valve. Steam came rushing out making a loud whistling sound, like the fog horn on a river boat.

"Grab the crosscut saw." The three men raced back up the hill. One of the men grabbed an ax and swiftly started chopping off the branches exposing the log pinning Lester to the ground. The other two set the saw blade on the tree trunk just two feet from Lester's body and started sawing desperately to relieve the pressure on their friend.

As soon as the blade cut through the tree trunk they threw the saw to one side and both men grabbed the exposed end of the tree trunk near Lester's boot and heaved the log up off him. Erick dropped his ax and knelt down to look at Lester, "He's still breathing, but he's hurt bad. Why don't you two run down and get a slab of lumber we can ease him over on and use it to carry him down to the wagon."

Taylor talked to Lester, "Hang on old buddy, we're gonna get you to town and the doc'll fix you up."

The other two ran back carrying a large slab of fresh cut wood about six foot long. It was just wide enough to roll the man over on it. They lifted him up and started down the hill moving as fast and as carefully as they could. Taylor pointed to the man supporting the middle of the board, "Turn loose and run down and get the team hooked to the wagon so it'll be ready to go when we get down there."

They got Lester loaded into the wagon then Taylor grabbed a piece of charcoal out of the fire and wrote on a fresh piece of wood and propped it up so Billy Joe would see it when he got back.

Tree fell on Lester gone to find a doctor.

CHAPTER TWENTY-ONE

"Russ, I want you to go to town and tell my lawyer I want to see him."

"Sure Joe. Do you want me to bring him back with me or can he come tomorrow if he is busy?"

"Unless he is in court bring him back with you. Just tell him I've got some stuff I want him to attend to."

Russ walked through the kitchen and said, "Joe wants me to go to town and bring back his lawyer. Do you have any idea what that's all about?"

"No. He may have some of them oilwell leases for him to look at."

Russ didn't push his horse, as far as he knew there was no hurry. He was enjoying the soft breeze and he watched a hawk glide silently across the sky looking for his dinner. A blue jay hopped from limb to limb of a tree he was passing under squawking at him. "Hush you loud mouth I'm not going to bother you."

A big old jackrabbit shot out of the weeds beside the road and raced down the road in front of him. Russ whistled through his teeth and the old rabbit stopped and his ears shot up. Russ laughed,

"He's trying to recognize the strange sound. I've got supper many times by doing that trick. You're safe today old rabbit. I'm going to get a lawyer. I don't have time to mess with you."

Russ inhaled deeply the sweet smell of the honeysuckle growing over the low shrubs down by the creek.

Later that afternoon Russ and the lawyer rode back into the yard at the Tumbling *C*. When they walked in Rosa said, "Good afternoon Mr. Lawton. Let me take your coat. Would you like a cup of coffee?"

"No thank you Rosa. Russ tells me you agreed to marry this galoot."

Russ said, "It was her cornbread. I was afraid if I didn't marry her some other dude would steal our cook."

"Russ you are pretty smart because I have eaten some of Rosa's cornbread and you were definitely running a risk." Turning back to Rosa he said, "How is Joe today?"

When the lawyer walked into Joe's bedroom he said, "Well I guess you know I was holding a winning hand and I cashed in when Russ came running in all out of breath saying you needed me right now."

"You old shyster, you can save your blarney for the court room. I probably saved you from losing this month's rent."

Lawton chuckled, "Hello Joe, what do you need?"

CHAPTER TWENTY-TWO

Mary Beth said, "Daddy, I wonder if that young man who rode with us for a ways back there in Texas, ever got up here and claimed some land."

"I noticed you kind-ah liked that cowboy. Unfortunately we'll probably never know. This is a big territory, if he's even here, he could be anywhere."

"If his daddy really owned all that land he claimed, then more than likely he decided to stay where he was."

"I know, but I was just wondering. After all no man could measure up to my daddy anyway."

"Mary Beth, your old daddy hasn't done too well by you yet. I sure hate to think of my daughter living in a sod house, I hear there's a sawmill over near Turner Falls. If we get a good crop this fall I plan to ride down there and buy enough lumber to start building a real house for you."

"Daddy, you know I don't care what kind of house we live in. If we get a good crop, I want us to buy some chickens and a milk cow."

"The next thing I'm gonna build is a smoke house so if I can get a buffalo and one of those wild hogs I can smoke the meat. That way we'll have meat all winter."

"My vegetable garden is doing well. We need to dig a root cellar. So I can put my produce in it as it gets ripe."

"Mary Beth, this is gonna be a good farm. All we need is three or four good crops and we'll build a nice house and barns. Then we'll find a good sturdy Christian man for your husband and someday you can get me some grandkids to make this old farm into a real home."

"Daddy, you can't just order up husbands and grandkids like you order seeds from a catalog."

⊨≒+ +≓⊨

Five miles south of the Crawford's, Snake and Leroy camped in a dry gulley.

"Snake, pickin's been pretty slim up here. These sod busters are all as broke as we are. Maybe we should ride on up to Kansas City and see if we can knock off a bank or something."

"Maybe we can catch one of them drovers who has just sold a bunch of longhorns and headin' back to Texas with his saddle bags full."

"Yeah, I need to find me a woman. With these scars on my face ever woman I look at won't even look back at me."

CHAPTER TWENTY-THREE

Billy Joe approached the saw mill. 'Something is wrong. I don't hear the saw. There is no smoke from the boiler.' He kicked B.J. in the ribs and the horse sprinted toward the saw mill.

As they drew closer it was obvious that everything was shut down. 'What's going on?'

When he jumped off the saddle he saw the note written on the piece of wood. 'Where would they go? Where would be the closest doctor? It's almost sundown, I can't go chasing off in the dark, I have no idea which way they went.'

Billy Joe decided it would be foolish to try to follow the wagon tracks because it would be dark soon. He tidied up the saw mill and fixed supper for himself. He was really worried about Lester. There was one thing about a saw mill, if you had an accident it normally was a bad accident.

The next morning he was up at sunrise. After sipping two cups of strong black coffee and chewing on a piece of hard tack he started the fire going under the boiler so they would have a head of steam by the time the crew got here.

Soon he looked up and two wagons pulled up. "Howdy. What can I do for you?"

"You the man selling lumber?"

"Yes sir, what do you need?"

The man pulled a note pad out of his bib overalls and asked, "Have you got any 2 by 4s and 1 by 8s, ten foot long?"

Pointing to stacks of lumber Billy Joe said, "I've got 2 by 4s and 1 by 8 siding all of 'em are ten foot long. How many do you need?"

Looking back at his note pad the man said, "I need sixty four of the 2 by 4s and one hundred of the 1 by 8s."

"Pull your wagon on up here and we'll load the 2 by 4s first so your load won't be top heavy. The 2 by 4s are a dollar and 1 by 8s are fifty cents."

The man on the wagon helped him load the lumber, and when they got through Billy Joe went back to the lumber pile and returned with one more of the two inch thick boards and two more of the one inch thick boards and loaded them on the wagon."

"Mister, what are you doing?" We already got what I asked for."

"Yes sir, but every time a man buys fifty boards, I always give him one extra just in case we miscounted."

The man reached back in his overalls and counted out one hundred and sixty dollars and said, "Mister I like doing business with an honest man. Thank ye."

Before that wagon got out of sight two more wagons ambled up to the mill.

When he was through loading the second wagon, two of his helpers came riding up.

CHAPTER TWENTY-FOUR

Joe Carville said, "I suspect I'm hurt worse than Rosa and them think, so here's what I want you to do. I want you to draw up a document giving a working interest in the Tumbling *C* to Rosa and Russ. The rest of the ranch I want to leave to my two granddaughters Caroline and Mattie."

"What about your grandson?"

"I ain't worried about that boy, he's just like his daddy. He'll make it just fine. I gave him my old saw mill. I'll bet a hundred dollars that right now he's making a fortune with that thing."

"Right now, I want to deed over to Russ and Rosa five acres of land around the house they've built. Then I want to fix my will,"

"Let me make sure I understand what you want. Before the will, you want to give them the house and five acres of land. That will be surveyed and deeded to them."

"Yes."

"In your will you want to leave Russ and Rosa a working share of the entire ranch."

"Yes."

"What about the oil wells?"

"They are part of the ranch aren't they?"

"If you say they are, yes."

"Then yes the oil wells are part of the ranch."

"You said working share. That needs to be better defined. Do you mean ten percent or twenty percent, what exactly is a working share?"

"Well they've both been with me for over twenty years so let's make it twenty-five percent."

"Joe that's a lot of money. Do you want to talk this over with Sam and Sally Jo before you sign it?"

"No. In fact if I know those two they will probably want me to give 'em even more. Are you worried about somebody contesting the will?"

"Sure, because when a lot on money is involved, people do strange things."

Joe looked at him and said, "Not this family. Sam wouldn't care if I gave the whole thing to the church, and Sally Jo would probably rather I gave it to some orphanage or something. Billy Joe knew all he had to do was stay home and someday he'd have both ranches. Instead he set out to make his own mark and he will. You mark my word, he will."

"If I don't get run over by a stampede or washed away in a flood I'll have this back for you next Monday."

"Don't mess around because I want to get this done. I don't want something to happen to me before you get this done so make this a priority."

"Joe I don't have a trial until the later part of next week so I'll get right on this."

"Lawton, there's one thing more I want you to do for me."

"Sure, Joe what's that?"

"Send the preacher out to see me."

Lawton looked at Joe and thought *maybe I'd better get this done as fast as I can.*

CHAPTER TWENTY-FIVE

"Hey guys. How's Lester doing?"

"He's broke up pretty bad. Leg's broke, ribs, doc kept him at the army post for now."

"We just came from his place. Did you know his misses and them kids are living in a dugout?"

"That's why he was working to get some lumber so he could build 'em a place to stay."

"We was wondering if you'd give him enough boards to build a little house?"

"We'll be glad to do the buildin' if you give him the lumber."

"I'll tell you what, you help me the rest of the week and come Saturday we'll all go over there and start putting up a house for them to bring him home to."

"If you'd do that we could get a few other fellows to help with the buildin'."

"As you can see I've just about sold out of all we've already got cut. So let's jump in and start cutting so we can take care of these other folks that are coming every day. Saturday morning y'all come on over here and bring your wagons. We'll load up enough to get a good start and then next Saturday we'll bring what else we need. If we can get some help we can probably get a place built in two weekends."

It was a little slower going since they were one man short. Billy Joe said, "Taylor why don't you run the saw. Jacob you stack lumber and Patrick you fell. I'll drag the logs down to the saw and when somebody comes to buy some lumber I'll wait on them. Jacob if I'm waiting on a customer and Taylor starts to run out of logs, you'll have-ta run up and snake a few down."

Every time a man ordered 100 boards Billy Joe gave him 102 just in case he miscounted. Soon his reputation grew, everybody said he was an honest man to do business with.

For the next three days they worked from sunup until sundown.

The Army Captain walked into the surgery center. "Button up any thing you've got going and start packing up your supplies. We just got orders to move out next Monday."

"Captain Burgess, I've got a problem. I have a man in here that a tree fell on. He is busted up pretty bad. I'm afraid if he spends the night outdoors he'll develop pneumonia and he will die. Can't you leave me and one nurse here for another week?"

"No. Our orders are specific, we're to move the entire command on Monday. Is he a military man?"

"No he's a civilian."

"Then there's no way the brass is gonna agree to splitting the unit. We'll be moving out in two days."

The doctor looked at Lester and thought, *well fellow I am gonna have to send you home in three days. I hope you've got a house already built.*

Jacob and Taylor rode by the field hospital to check on Lester on Friday on their way home. He didn't look too good. As they were leaving they stopped and talked to the doctor.

"Doc, how's he doing? He don't look to good."

"He's bad hurt. I suspect he'll pull through if he doesn't come down with an infection. We're keeping him warm and dry in here, but we just got orders to pull out at first light Monday morning. So we're gonna have-ta leave him behind. I hope he's got a good tight house to go to because if he gets chilled in his condition I'm afraid he'll come down with pneumonia and that'll kill 'em."

Jacob looked at Taylor and said. "We got some work to do."

On Saturday morning two wagons rolled up to the saw mill as the sun was just peeping over the ridge in the east. Billy Joe had his wagon already loaded with lumber and a fire going, "Step down and have some coffee then we'll load your wagons. We don't have many nails so I stayed up last night and whittled a bunch of dowel pins."

As they stood around the fire drinking strong black coffee, Jacob told Billy Joe what the doctor had said.

"Let's get those wagons loaded. I've been telling everybody who came and bought lumber this week about what we were going to do. Several said they would come and help. I hope they do. If we get enough men working, we can put up a tight house in two days."

"Taylor, do they have a spring or a creek close by?"

"I only been there once or twice, I never paid any attention."

"We can't bring him home to a dugout in his condition. Especially the way them clouds are a-gathering up way out west, there may be a storm here by Monday."

"I've loaded some 2 by 8s on my wagon so we can use them for floor joists. I brought enough to make a twenty by twenty floor. We can get a couple of men to building the floor and a couple of more building walls. When the floor's done we can stand the walls up on the floor and pin 'em together then two men can start slapping siding on. We can then put two men to framing the roof. The siding can then go right on up over the top and that house will be pretty much in the dry."

"We can always stretch a wagon sheet over the roof and nail it down around the edges."

"Fellows we'll just pray it don't come a storm before we get that done."

For the next several hours men sweated, saws rang and hammers pounded a rhythm as the frame of the house took shape. Billy Joe kept glancing at a dark stormy cloud that appeared to be closer every time he looked at it. By sundown Billy Joe said, "Fellows it's getting too dangerous to work any longer. Those that can let's bed down right here. The rest of you, if you could, try to be here at first light we might have the house in the dry before that thing gets here."

All eyes looked to the northwest and occasional streaks of lightening could be seen on the horizon.

By mid-morning the wind was picking up, making the building even more dangerous, especially for those up on the roof. Not one man threatened to quit, especially with a young mother and three little children huddled on the lee side of the dugout watching their gallant effort. They had used up all of the nails in erecting the frame. Two men would hold a long 1 by 8 plank up in place and two men with awls were boring holes through the 1 by 8 plank and into the 2 by 8 frame. It was slow painful work but as soon as the holes were finished two other men with wooden pegs started pounding them into the new holes. As soon as they had pegs at each end of the 1 by 8 the men holding the board would turn loose of that one and reach for a new board.

By noon they had the siding on, up to the eve of the roof. They then built homemade ladders by cutting notches in two long 2 by 8 boards and fitting two-foot-long boards in the notches forming steps to climb up to the roof.

When the first man climbed up his ladder the wind blew it off the side of the house. He managed to jump free and they were lucky the heavy wooden ladder didn't hit anyone on the ground.

"Hold it, we will have-ta secure those ladders." Billy Joe said. "Somebody get me some rope."

One of the men handed Billy Joe some rope, "I need three of you to hold this ladder up against the house while I climb up there and tie it to the rafters."

As soon as they stood the ladder up a strong gust of wind almost jerked it out of their hands.

"Billy Joe, you can't climb up there it'll kill ya."

Billy Joe didn't say a word he just pointed to the buckboard pulling into the yard. They all watched as the young mother and her children ran to the back of the buckboard.

"Okay guys let's get this done for them."

Four strong men forced the ladder against the siding they had just put on the house. As soon as the ladder touched the side of the house Billy Joe was climbing it as fast as he could. He felt the first drops of rain hit his arm.

CHAPTER TWENTY-SIX

L awton showed up Sunday afternoon with a man from the bank
with him, "Joe you remember Swisher from the bank? I brought
him along so he could notarize you signing these documents. That
makes them official in any court of law."

Joe was wheezing as he sat up on the side of the bed, "Lawton
I'm glad you made it back. Mr. Swisher, I appreciate you coming
out to do this for us."

"Joe I want you to sign right on the line where I put the X." He
pointed to the X on each piece of paper. As soon as Joe signed one
Lawton handed it over to Swisher who put his stamp on it and then
signed it himself.

When they were finished Lawton placed the signed documents
in a leather folder and handed one to Joe and kept on for himself.
"Joe do you want me to get Russ and Rosa to come in here so you
can give them the deed or do you want to wait until y'all are by
yourselves?"

"Right now, I just want to lay back down in this bed. You hold
on to 'em and in the next few days I'll send them to town and you
can give it to them."

"Well Joe, me and Swisher better be getting back to town. It looks like a big storm is moving down from the northwest. All of the old timers are saying this 'en looks like it's gonna be a frog strangler."

As they started to get in the buggy Swisher looked off to the northwest and said, "Those people up there in the Oklahoma Territory better have a good place to hunker down, cause by this time tomorrow they're gonna be in it for sure."

⇒⊣⊢⇐

One mile south of the Carpenters, Snake and Leroy topped a ridge as a brilliant streak of lightening flashed across the sky. Leroy said, "Snake we better find us a cave or something to holdup in."

"I ain't holding up in no cold wet cave. I'm gonna find one of these sod busters who has built a nice warm dry cabin, and maybe he'll even have a woman in it."

Up on the next ridge they spotted smoke coming from a chimney about a mile west of where they were sitting. Snake pointed.

Jon Yoder was just leaving the three-sided lean to he had erected to shelter his milk cow and the two mules when two men rode up.

"What are you some kind of gambler? What are you doing out here in the middle of nowhere?" Snake asked.

"No, my name is Jon Yoder. May I ask why you would think of me as a gambler?"

"What are you lookin' at?"

"I am sorry I meant no disrespect. You appear to have been injured."

"If you look at my face again you are going to be injured."

"If you're not a gambler are you a preacher?"

"No. My name is Jon Yoder, this is my farm, that the Lord has given me to work. What can I do for you gentlemen?"

"Well you've got on those black pants and that white shirt and them suspenders and that flat black hat. If you ain't a gambler or a sky pilot, what are ye?"

"I am Amish"

"Have you got any grub around here?" Snake was eyeing the place up, he didn't see any sign of a woman around,

"Yes, earlier the Lord brought me a deer near where I was working so I harvested it. I have potatoes that I have already dug. We can have plenty of meat and potatoes."

"I'm gonna put our horses in that lean to."

"Jake and Jon and Elsie won't mind sharing the shelter until after the storm has passed. It will be tight but they won't mind."

"They won't mind. I don't care how much those dumb brutes mind I'm putting my horse in that shelter."

"Do not speak of the Lord's beast of burdens that way. The Lord has provided them to help us with our labors."

CHAPTER TWENTY-SEVEN

"Mary Beth, that berry pie was the best I have ever had."
"I found a good patch down by the creek. I was looking at the wheat today. It looks good."

"Yeah, honey if this storm doesn't beat it down we'll have good crop. Then we'll go find that man who is selling lumber and see if we can get enough to build a real house. One with a wood floor in it."

"Oh, daddy you really are trying to spoil me. How will I ever find a husband who has a wood floor in his house, out here in the territory?"

"If you find the right fellow, I'll help him build you a new house with a wood floor and everything you want in it. If it'll help get me some grandkids to bounce on my knee when I get old."

"Well daddy first of all I haven't found a husband yet, and second you are not old enough to sit and bounce grandkids on your knee."

"Mary Beth sometimes I wish your mother could be here to see you now, she would be so proud of you. You had a wonderful mother and someday I know you will be a wonderful mother just like she was."

"I hear tell a traveling preacher is setting up a brush arbor over east of here and starting next Sunday he'll be preaching for about ten days. Do you want-ta go hear him?"

"Yes daddy, I would like that. I need to hear some preaching and it will be a chance for us to meet some more of our neighbors. "

At the Sunday meeting they met several of their new neighbors. A pact was made between several of the wheat farmers to help each other gather their crops before winter set in.

"Mary Beth, a buyer has set up a trading post in a community called Guthrie. It's about a day's drive southeast of the farm. We'll take a wagon load down there tomorrow. I understand the man selling lumber is about two days south of Guthrie so we'll mosey on down there and bring back a wagon load of lumber. I figure it'll take about three trips to sell all the wheat and each time we do we'll bring back a load of lumber. I already talked to three or four of the neighbors about helping me build the house. So we'll probably have to spend another winter in the sod house. Then next spring we'll have to put in another crop. As soon as the plantings done we'll finish the new house and move in."

"Daddy, can we go down to the creek and dig up a couple of young sapling trees to plant around the house, so we'll have shade?"

"Sure we can and I saw some wild roses growing over near the spring. We can get a couple of cuttings off of them and stick 'em in a fruit jar full of water until they grow roots then we can plant them if you want to."

CHAPTER TWENTY- EIGHT

The men had just gotten the last dowel pins holding the last board on the roof when the rain started falling. Of course the water dripped through the cracks between the raw boards no matter how tight the men tried to force them together.

"Billy Joe this will never do. They can't live in this house until we can get shingles on that roof."

"You're right. I've got a big wagon sheet in my wagon. Let's stretch that tarpaulin over the roof until we can come back and put shingles on it."

"Billy Joe have we got any nails left?"

"I don't know? Does anybody have any small nails left?"

"Yeah I got a hand full in my tool apron." Patrick said.

"This darn thing is too heavy to lift up there especially with it raining on it."

"Jacob, grab somebody to help ya and lay two of those 2 by 8s up against the edge of the roof and see if you can hold them there. Two of you other guys bring that roll of tarpaulin around here. One of you other guys get a lariat rope and see if you can throw it over the house to us. We'll tie the end of it around the tarpaulin and once we get it tied everybody, except the two holding the planks up against the house, run around there and see if we can pull it up to the roof."

With a lot of grunting and sweating they soon had the heavy roll up on the top of the house.

"Okay let's leave it rolled up. Taylor you follow me. We'll get up there and one on each side of the peak we'll nail down the edge of the tarpaulin then we'll slowly unroll it along the ridge line nailing it down as we go. The boards were wet and slick. Taylor slipped and started to slide off the roof. Billy Joe reached out and grabbed his pant leg just before he went over the edge. He felt the weight of Taylor pulling him off the roof. He knew if he let go the man was dead. If he didn't let go they could both be dead.

Billy Joe slapped the palm of his hand on the slick board deck trying to stop the slide. He could see that Taylor was only three feet from going over the side. Billy Joe felt his body slowly slipping toward the edge of the building. Frantically with his free hand he grabbed the tarpaulin. It was wet. His hand slid off. Desperately he grasped for anything that he could grab a hold on to. Taylor moved and they slid down another foot closer to the edge.

Taylor was starting to panic, he was less than two feet from the edge and the rain was coming down harder. Billy Joe's fingers grasped the rope attached to the tarpaulin and it too started to slide off the top of the house.

Screaming at the top of his voice Billy Joe yelled, "Pull the rope. Pull us back up." Slowly he felt the rope grow taught and ever so slowly he felt his body being pulled back up to the point of the roof. Soon he was able to flip over on the opposite side of the roof and reach Taylor's hand spinning him around so that his head was toward the ridge instead of the edge. The two men lay there on each side of the roof ridge clasping each other's hands. It took a moment for them to regain their breath.

"Somebody throw me another rope up here."

"Billy Joe what are you going to do with another rope?"

"I'm gonna tie me and Taylor together. If he works on that side of the ridge and I stay on this side neither one of us should slip and fall off the house. Patrick why don't you climb up here and get on the point of the ridge and help us unroll the tarp. For goodness sake be careful I don't want to go through that again."

In about a half hour the three men had the canvas tarpaulin in place and nailed down.

The rain stopped just before they were ready to climb down. Three soaking wet roofers were happy to be on the ground. One of the neighbors said, "Come in and dry out I've got a good fire started."

Two others came in bringing Lester and his family. They spread blankets on the floor and laid him gently near the fireplace. "Lester you'll be comfortable there until we can get your bed moved in."

Billy Joe looked around at the house they had built. It was solid built, the siding on the outside was solid 1 by 8 planks. The inner walls were solid 1 by 8 planks fitted tightly together, creating a dead air space between the inner wall and the siding on the outside. "Taylor, it is dry and it should be easy to keep it warm with the double walls. Can you see the door?"

"Yes."

"See that long plank hanging in the middle of the door?"

"Yeah."

"It is hanging by a big pin in the middle. Every night you simply turn that piece of wood across the door and it will cover the door facing on each side. That is your lock, nobody can open that door until you turn that wooden button back like it is now."

"If someone tries to attack the house, do you see those small pieces of wood attached to the door?"

"Yeah."

"They'll turn like the big one. They cover a gun port. You simply turn the lock and it will open up a hole for you to poke out a gun and shoot without opening the door."

"I appreciate it Billy Joe but I doubt I'll ever need that. All of my neighbors helped build this. I can't tell all of ya how grateful I am."

"Lester, I hope you don't ever need it either but there are still some bad dudes running around out there."

"Billy Joe, I don't know how to thank you. I'll be back to work as soon as I can."

"Ma'am do you need anything for you and the kids?"

"No, thank you so much. We've got vegetables from the garden in the dugout and Lester killed a boar just before the tree fell on him, and smoked the meat."

"Lester, me or one of the fellows will stop by from time to time, but if you ever need anything you send one of the young'uns running over to the sawmill."

"I will."

Billy Joe slipped on his coat and said, "Ya'll be safe now. You've had enough bad luck. As soon as we can we'll come back and replace that canvas tarpaulin with shingles."

CHAPTER TWENTY-NINE

Three dirty straggly looking men rode up to Jon Yoder's place and Snake stepped out to meet them. "Hello boys where have you been? We've been looking for ya."

"We've been looking for you. Took us a while to track you down. The whisky peddler told us you were here."

"I hope ya brought some more, we're just about out."

One of the men reached into his saddle bag and pulled out a large jug.

A tired sweaty Jon Yoder came in from the field and was surprised to find three more men sitting around his table drinking whisky and playing cards.

"I do not want whiskey in my house. This is the Lord's house, we do not want cards and whisky in this house."

"Flathead get something straight. This ain't your house and it ain't the lord's house any more. It's my house and these are my friends. If you don't like it you can move or you can get you a gun and we'll settle who owns this house right now. In fact I want to see that deed the government man gave you."

"Why do you want to see my deed?"

"Because, you are gonna sign it over to me right now."

"I raced for this land, I built this house with my own hands. I will not sign it over to you."

Snake swung his hardened fist and hit Yoder in the face knocking him back out the door. Before Yoder could get back to his feet Snake jumped on him and started kicking him in the stomach and ribs.

Leroy said, "Whoa, Snake don't kill 'em we need him to milk the cow and cook for us."

Snake spat on Yoder and walked back into the house. Yoder lay writhing in pain his blood soaking into the sand from the cuts he had received.

"Here's what I've been thinking boys. Do you see that grain out there in the field? Now we could help our friend Yoder go out there and harvest all of that grain and go sell it. But I have a better idea. All these flatland farmers will be hauling their wagons loaded with grain down to that trader in Guthrie. We'll let them pick it and haul it and we'll catch 'em on the way back and take the money from 'em."

"That's a lot better idea than us being out there breaking our backs picking that stuff. Snake, I like the way you think. Pass that jug back over here. We just need to get us some women out here."

CHAPTER THIRTY

Mary Beth was driving one wagon, following her dad in the other. Both wagons were loaded with grain from the harvest as they rode into the grain yard in Guthrie.

One hour later they were through unloading the grain. The grain trader said, "Mr. Carpenter that's good looking grain. I'm paying you top price. You must have good soil where you're farming. I'll look forward to seeing you next year. I need to warn you. Last week a man sold me a bunch of grain and got robbed on the way home. A bunch of masked men took every penny of the money I'd paid him."

As they walked back to the wagons Mr. Carpenter said, "Mary Beth he paid us seven hundred dollars. We can go on down to the lumber mill and buy enough lumber to build the first stage of the house we designed."

"Oh, Daddy do you think we can get it built before winter returns?"

"I think so, we still have a little money left, so maybe we can hire a couple of men to help with the building."

"Daddy have you seen anything of Mr. Yoder? I wonder if he got his grain gathered."

"Mary Beth, I don't know. It would be neighborly of us to stop in and check on him on the way back home."

Late that afternoon they pulled into Billy Joe's lumber yard.

Mary Beth was the first one to recognize Billy Joe. They were sitting on the wagon seats with the sun to their backs as Billy Joe walked toward them. With the sun in his eyes he could only make out that two wagons had arrived and each wagon had one person on the seat. "Oh, Daddy look."

Charles Carpenter asked, "Are you the young man who rode with us a few miles back in Texas?"

"Yes sir, I am. Where's your farm? I looked all over for you when we started? How did I miss you?"

"Daddy moved on up and entered from the Kansas side. Our farm is Northwest of Guthrie."

"Well it's good to see you again. Please come. I'm sorry I've been so busy selling lumber I haven't had time to build anything but this little shack that serves as my office and sleeping quarters. At least I do have a stove and right now I've got some stew that has been simmering all day. I just put a pan of corn bread in the Dutch oven. It'll be ready in a few minutes. Mr. Carpenter, how was this year's crop?"

"The Lord blessed us. We had a very good crop. I promised Mary Beth that if we had a good crop we would come down and buy enough lumber to build a real house before winter sets in."

Billy Joe helped Mr. Carpenter unhook the teams and lead them to water. He said, "Sir I would like your permission to court your daughter. I've been looking for y'all ever since I met you on the trail back down in Texas."

Mr. Carpenter stopped and looked at him, "Exactly what are your intentions young man?"

"Well sir as you can see I've got a pretty good business going here so I can support a wife and family. So, after she gets to know me better I would like to ask Mary Beth to marry me, and someday we'll bring you some grandchildren."

"Son you realize, that she may have a different idea. You can court her and you can ask her but if she says no, then it's no. Do you agree?"

"Yes sir, I'll take my chances."

After supper Mr. Carpenter said, "I hope you don't mind, but I'm all tuckered out. Y'all won't wander off and get in no trouble if I turn in will ya?"

"No daddy we're not going to go wandering off. Good night."

The fires in the boiler were winding down. Billy Joe pointed to a big log theyhad pulled up ready to mount on the trundle in the morning. "We can sit here. It's so peaceful at night I like to sit here and look at all the stars."

"It is beautiful out here. The sky is jet black and the stars look like you could reach up and touch them. Even the clicking and popping of the metal on your boiler cooling down is a peaceful sound."

"Y'all must've had a good crop."

"It was very good, we have good soil and the rains came just right. That's why we're here. We want to buy enough lumber to build a proper house."

"That's what your pa said. Where did you stay last winter?"

"Daddy cut blocks of sod and built a sod house. It was pretty easy to keep warm because the sod blocks were about two feet thick. It was kind of like living in a cave. I look forward to having a real floor to sweep."

While they were talking Billy Joe had picked up a scrap of wood and using his pocket knife started to whittle. "How close is your closest neighbor?"

"The closest is Mr. Yoder. We haven't seen him lately. I guess he is busy getting his wheat harvested. He is an Amish man. Keeps a good farm. Daddy and I were talking about stopping in to see him on the way home to see if he needed any help getting his crops in."

CHAPTER THIRTY-ONE

The next morning at breakfast, Mary Beth had found some eggs in a sage hen's nest, "While you two figure out how much lumber we're gonna need I'll scramble these and fry up some bacon."

"Mr. Carpenter, I would make the kitchen on one end of the house and the sleeping rooms on the other. Cause in the summer that kitchen will get real hot."

"Yeah, we'll build in lots of windows that can let the breeze blow in.'

"We can make shutters that can be closed in the winter or in the case of an Indian attack. I always build them with port holes for shooting out if you need to."

"Yeah, we can always hang a block of wood over them to keep the cold wind out. Hang it in such a way that you can move out of the way if you have to shoot out through the hole."

"It ain't just Indians you've got to worry about out here. There have been several farms raided in the last few months and the whole family killed."

"Billy Joe, we need to set up some kind of local government and get us a local sheriff out here."

"Several of my neighbors' have been around talking about that. They asked me to be the sheriff for this area, but I'm too busy cutting wood."

After breakfast they were sitting around drinking coffee when Billy Joe said, "Mr. Carpenter, Mary Beth and I talked a long time last night, and we'd like to get married next spring."

Mr. Carpenter looked at Mary Beth and said, "That's a pretty quick decision on something as important as the rest of your life."

"I know daddy, but I thought the first time I met Billy Joe, he was special. Now I know he is. Of course a girl can always change her mind between now and next spring if he starts misbehaving." She smiled.

"Mr. Carpenter, I would like to come with you and bring a couple of my men to help you build the house. Working together we can get a house built pretty quick. After all I don't want my future wife to have-ta spend another winter living in a sod house when her husband owns a lumber mill."

"Billy Joe, whose gonna run the mill while you are gone."

"I'll leave a couple of men here to keep it going. We won't be gone more than a week or so."

They loaded the wagon Mr. Carpenter would be driving with 2 by 8 inch lengths of lumber and 2 by 4 inch lengths. Billy Joe explained that they would build the outside walls out of 2 by 8 boards to allow more "dead air" space between the inner wall and the outside wall. The dividing inner walls would be made of 2 by 4 pieces of lumber. The second wagon would be driven by Billy Joe, with Mary Beth riding with him would be filled with 1 by 8 pieces of lumber to be used for decking the floors and siding on the outer walls and roof. The third wagon would be driven by one of the men and it would be filled with shingles for the roof, nails, and hinges.

Ponderously the heavy loaded wagons rolled north on the third day. As they rolled slowly across the hills and plains Mary Beth and Billy Joe had a chance to talk and plan.

"Billy Joe, tell me about your family."

"Well my mother died when I was born, her name was Mattie Ann, of course I never knew her. I understand she was very pretty. Her cousin Sally Jo took me in to care for as soon as I was born. She lived with my grandpa, Joe Carville, who was her uncle. Then when I was about two years old my pa married Sally Jo and she is the only mother I ever knew and she is wonderful, you will love her. I have two younger sisters, one is thirteen years old and the other is ten years old. They both go to the local school.

"Didn't you tell me your daddy owned a large ranch?"

"Yes, he owns the W-F and my grandpa owns the Tumbling C."

"What did your parents think when you told them you wanted to come to Oklahoma and start a saw mill?"

"They wanted me to go to college and come back and help run the family business. So, we made a deal, they would agree to let me go for two years. If I did not have a good farm going at the end of two years I was going to come back home and go to college. I didn't plan on opening a saw mill. I chose the plot of land with a gap into the hill because there is a beautiful valley back in the mountain that can only be gotten to by going through that gap and since I now own the gap I am the only one with access to the valley. My idea was to raise cattle in the valley"

Mary Ruth laughed, "So by choosing the one hundred and sixty acres you actually have use of a lot more land on which to raise cattle. What happened to the cattle idea?"

"I felled a few logs to build a cabin on the cleared spot where the mill sits. Before I had a chance to start building the cabin, two men came and offered to buy the logs from me for ten dollars a log. The first week I was here I sold twenty logs. I made $200.00 dollars. I thought if I had a saw mill I could get a lot more than $10.00 per log. Then I remembered my grandpa had an old saw mill out behind his barn. So I went home and asked grandpa to sell it to me. Instead he gave it to me and I came back and started sawing lumber. Every time a customer came to buy lumber I asked them if they knew where Mr. Carpenter settled. I was still looking for you."

"Awe, that is sweet. I never stopped thinking about you. I had decided that you probably never came, that you probably decided to stay on the ranch. I'm glad you didn't." As she hugged his left arm.

"Mary Beth, we'll get a fine house built for your pa, then I'll go back and start building a home for us. You will need to come as often as you can to see what I'm building and tell me what you want in it."

She snuggled up against him and said, "Billy Joe it is going to be so grand, we'll have children and daddy will have grandchildren."

"Next spring I'll take you down to meet pa and mom, and grandpa, and Russ and Rosa, the whole bunch they're gonna love you."

"Billy Joe, life is so good and it's going to be even better when we are a family. I can hardly wait until spring."

CHAPTER THIRTY-TWO

"Set those stones for the corners first. Balance a 2 by 8 from one corner stone to the next. It is important that we get the frame exactly level for the floor because if that is even a tiny bit off it will throw the whole structure off." Mr. Carpenter said, "Now Mary Beth bring me a clear glass bowl full of water."

Billy Joe and one of the other men looked at each other and then shrugged.

"Mr. Carpenter took the bowl from Mary Beth's hands and very carefully set it in the middle of the 2 by 8 halfway between the corner rocks. "Fellows we're a tiny bit low on that side," pointing to his left. Take one of them shingles and gently push it under the board until I tell you to stop."

Billy Joe took a shingle and slowly started forcing it under the 2 by 8 plank between the board and the rock. Soon it reached a point when he couldn't push it any farther.

Mr. Carpenter said, "Take a hammer and tap it very gently until the water in this bowl is level."

Billy Joe gently tapped the end of the shingle.

On the third tap Mr. Carpenter said, "That's enough. We're level. Now Billy Joe saw off the rest of the shingle, don't leave any sticking out to catch rain or snow."

By noon they had the frame for the floor level. During lunch Billy Joe said, "Mr. Carpenter why don't we let two of these men start nailing down the floor boards and the rest of us will start nailing together the frames for the walls."

"That sounds like a good idea." He pointed to two men setting across from where he and Billy Joe were sitting, "Why don't you guys get the deck nailed down. Billy Joe why don't you two start nailing the frames together. While you're doing that I'll start framing the doors. I might even get the window frames made before dark."

The five men worked tirelessly all day and by night fall they had the entire frame of a new home standing.

While the men were building Mary Beth had been working to put together supper for five very tired hungry men. She had a big blacked iron pot hanging over the fire with beans and bacon, bubbling and giving off a delicious aroma.

She had scrounged around and found squaw cabbage growing in the ravine. She had dumped some bacon grease in the cabbage that she had saved from breakfast. She had potatoes that they had brought with them and rubbed bacon grease all over them then buried the potatoes in the hot ash of the fire then raked burring coals over the ash. Then she mixed up a big batch of cornbread and filled an iron Dutch oven and placed it on the burning coals.

As the men laid down their tools and looked around they were surprised, Mary Beth had taken two saw horses and laid three long 1 by 8 boards across them making a make shift table. On the table she had set a steaming hot pan of cornbread, a large serving bowl of beans and ham, a large serving bowl of squaw cabbage and huge platter of baked potatoes. She had drug two stumps up on each side of her make shift table and laid two long 2 by 8 boards on them to form two benches for the men to sit on.

Billy Joe said, "Wow men. I think we're going to be dining in style tonight look at that."

Mary Beth standing to one side felt her face starting to feel flush. Her pa walked over and put his arm around her and said, "Honey you've made me proud. This is much better than any of us was expecting." His remarks were followed by a bunch of fellows saying amen.

Mary Beth said, "You men sit down, I am going to wait until you are all served before I sit down in case I have to refill one of the bowls or something."

While the happy crew was enjoying the Carpenter's first meal at their new home, eight hungry, hung over, and a half-drunk scar faced man and his crew were sixty miles south of Kansas City winding their way back to Jon Yoder's farm.

CHAPTER THIRTY-THREE

On the evening of the fourth night at the new home Billy Joe and Mary Beth walked out and sat on the tail gate of one of the wagons. His desire to take her in his arms was so strong he felt his nerves tingling all through his body. He had difficulty controlling his breathing.

Mary Beth thought *I know we should wait until next spring when we are married but my desire is so strong, I can't stand it. I love this man so much.*

Billy Joe kissed her and she responded passionately. The embrace grew longer and more passionate. The fire blew out of control in both of them.

All at once a voice said, "Excuse me. Can I trouble you for a drink of cold water?"

Billy Joe whipped around and reached for his six-shooter, there stood and old emaciated looking Indian. *Where did he come from? He looks like he could use a cup of water.*

Billy Joe was still standing there with his blood boiling in his veins. *I don't know whether to shoot that old man or thank him. I know two things, it's going to be a long time until spring and we have got to be more careful. If that old Indian hadn't come when he did—I'm just glad he did. I still don't know where he came from.*

The next morning Billy Joe and the men from the mill loaded their tools in the wagon. After breakfast, Mr. Carpenter said, "Billy Joe and all you men from the mill, I don't know the words to thank you enough for all you've done."

"Are you sure you don't need us to stay and help you build the doors and window shutters?"

"I really thank you guys for building that nice clean outhouse. Thank you." Mary Beth said.

Billy Joe walked over to Mary Beth and hugged her, "I'll be back as often as I can. I'll start building a house as soon as I get back. You'll need to get your father to bring you down in a few weeks to make sure I'm building what you want."

"Billy Joe if you build it, I will love it."

Mr. Yoder was struggling to lift the basket full of wheat up to pour the grains of wheat into the wagon box, the pain in his ribs was almost unbearable. He was certain that at least two ribs were broken from the kicks he received from Snake.

He looked up to the sky and said, "Lord, I am sorry but I need your help. The pain makes me weak. I know I must get the wheat harvested before the men return. Please help me."

All at once a withered brown hand reached over his shoulder and pushed the basket up over the edge of the wagon box. Startled Yoder looked to see who it was. An old Indian stood beside him, and as Yoder looked he saw several other Indians cutting wheat in his field.

"My friend, perhaps you could use some help, the tribe can use some flour, could we help you and you could pay us by giving us some of the grain to make flour for the papooses?"

"Thank you sir, I was just asking the Lord to send me some help."

"He heard." The old Indian said.

By the end of the day the job of harvesting that would have taken a healthy man a week to do was done. Mr. Yoder poured a bushel of wheat into bags and gave each man a bag saying, "Thank you so much. I could not have done this harvest without you."

The men grunted and said something in Apache, hefted the bags on their shoulders and walked away. Mr. Yoder turned to thank the old Indian and he was not there. "Where did he go? He didn't walk with them."

The sun was slowly sinking in the west when two dusty, creaking wagons rolled into the yard at the saw mill. Four tired weary loggers started stripping the harness off the mules.

The sun was painting silver and blue patterns in the eastern sky when Billy Joe opened his eyes. He sat up and pulled on his boots. Busied himself getting a fire going for coffee and breakfast, I have-ta get moving, gotta get the fire going in the boilers, the guys will be here in a few minutes. We've got a lot of cuttin' to do, to make up for the days we were gone.

The hills around the saw mill were absolutely beautiful, the leaves were splashed with dazzling colors, bright orange, to gold, to sunshine yellow with the dark green cedars splashed in to add contrast. Billy Joe stood staring at the beauty of God's handy work. It was so pretty he wanted to stop cutting until the leaves fell, but he had orders to fill.

Then one morning Billy Joe woke to find a dazzling white blanket four inches thick covering everything. The beautiful fall colors were gone, replaced by a clean pure white blanket of new fallen snow. Walking out of the shack they had put together for an office and sleeping room, there was not a track on the snow it was unblemished. The sun rays were peeping over the ridge to the east, glistening off the snow, it looked like a million diamonds sparkling on the side of the hill. They had been cutting and delivering timber as fast as they could, but he knew there were many people out there living in dugouts and root cellars still.

Jacob and Patrick rode up and stepped down. "Morning fellows, I don't think we'll be delivering any lumber today."

"No I suspect most of the building is done for this year." Patrick said, "If you don't need me, I've got some building I need to do at my place. "

"Well since you're already here, why don't we work today putting up drying sheds so we can keep most of the rain and snow off the green lumber."

"What are you figerin' about twenty feet deep and one-hundred feet long?"

"Yeah, let's go fell about fifteen long slender saplings for support posts We'll build them with flat roofs that are slightly higher in the front so the water will shed off to the back."

Even though the temperature had to be in the twenties the sun was shining bright and clear and when they started swinging those axes soon they were shedding their heavy coats. When the coats came off you could see, each man was wearing a forty-four on his hip. By noon they had fifteen trees cut, trimmed and hauled down to the area they intended to erect the drying shed.

"Whoa, what is that? Taylor asked.

They all looked and coming toward them was a rickety looking homemade sled pulled by an old gray mule.

Bill Joe stepped out to meet them, "Yes sir what can I do for you?"

"Me and my boy here come to see if we could get any kindling off of ya. We've been heatin' the dugout with buffalo chips but now they're all wet."

"How far did you fellows come?"

"I figure about thirty miles as the crow flies. We had heard you was running a saw mill over here and we was hoping we could kinda help you clean up the scraps and use them for fire wood."

Bill Joe stuck out his hand and said, "My name is Billy Joe McClanton, these three fellows work with me here at the mill, that's Jacob, Taylor and Patrick. Last night before I turned in, I put a big old pot of beans on the fire with the ham hock of a big old boar I killed a while ago so they orta be ready for us to eat by now, You fellows come in and eat some beans with us then we'll help you gather up all the kinlin' you can haul."

"My name is Earl Suggs and this is my boy Paul but we all call him Rooster."

"Well come on in and let's see if those beans are ready."

When they were all around the table Billy Joe had built in the office and sleeping room, he bowed his head and said, ***"Lord we thank you for these blessings we are about to partake in. Lord I pray you'll give all these men safe passage back to their homes.***

In Jesus name,

Amen

"Mr. Suggs how are things over in ya'll's area?"

"It's pretty bad, me and several others had a pretty good crop but highway men took all the money from us before we got back home with it. Now those same guys are coming around saying they'll protect us from other robbers next year but we've got to agree to give them half of all we collect. So basically we're all share croppers on our on places. We had it better than this back in Mississippi at least we had a house to live in, the landlord furnished a house. They done killed one of our neighbors cause he told 'em he wasn't going to go along with 'em. He has two nearly grown boys so I guess next spring they'll be plantin'."

"How many is in that bunch?"

"There's about six or seven. The main one's got a bad scared up face, he is plain bad around the women folks, I hear he took one fellow's wife home with 'em. They pistol whipped her husband and left him lying in the yard and took off taking his wife with 'em."

Billy Joe knew who the scar faced bandit was, so he immediately thought about Mary Beth and her pa.

CHAPTER THIRTY-FOUR

The sun was not yet over the east ridge when Billy Joe threw the saddle on BJ. "I hope you are ready to cover some ground. I need to go make sure Mary Beth and her dad are okay."

The big buckskin snorted and pawed the ground with his right front hoof.

I left Jacob in charge,, he can handle any business that comes along while I am gone.

Billy Joe loved to be up and traveling early in the morning. He loved the fresh clean smell of pine trees and sage in the air, in the early dawn light everything looked clean and fresh. As he rode along he reached down and pulled out his six-shooter to check the loads. "I have a funny feeling I may need this thing before long." Then he slipped the Winchester out of its scabbard and checked the loads.

He had gone about a mile when they came to a creek cut into the side of the hill. Billy Joe gave B.J. his reins and allowed the horse to choose its own pace going down into the water. He loved the feeling of power in those big muscles when he slid back into the cantle of the saddle as B.J. bounded up the other side of the bank in six long strides.

Winter would be coming on soon, all the leaves were off the trees, the air had a crisp feel this morning. He would really enjoy this ride today if it weren't for the uneasy feeling that something was wrong at Mary Beth's place.

Jacob was running the saw when he looked up as a buggy pulled into the yard. He noticed that it was occupied by two well-dressed men. He shut the loud saw down and said, "Howdy. What can I do for you gentlemen?"

"Are you the owner?"

"No sir, he will be gone for a few days, can I help you?"

"No sir we need to talk to him. When is he expected back?"

"Sir I'm not sure. I expect it'll be a week to ten days."

The man handed Jacob a business card that said, Miles Cafton, attorney at law, general delivery Ardmore Oklahoma, on it. "Who is the owner of this mill?"

"Billy Joe McClanton."

"Please see that he gets my card when he returns. Tell him we need to talk with him as soon as possible after he returns from this trip."

"Yes sir, I'll see that he gets your card."

Snake and his men were coming back after one of their raids when he happened to ride out of the tree line and spotted Mary Beth hanging her washing on the line to dry.

One of the outlaws said, "Boss, do you want us to ride down there and see if they have anything we need?"

Snake sat watching Mary Beth, he thought that is one pretty woman. "Naw, y'all go ahead I'm gonna watch this one a minute." *That is a classy woman. She would make a classy looking wife.* He reached up and touched his face.

CHAPTER THIRTY-FIVE

Late in the afternoon the wind started to pick up and clouds began to roll in. Sleet started to sting Billy Joe's face. "B.J. we need to find some shelter this could be a bad storm." He reached back and pulled his Buffalo skin coat from behind the saddle. The sleet turned into hail as the pellets grew larger.

Billy Joe turned B.J. into the trees to give them some protection in case the hail stones grew larger. "B.J. we have got to find some shelter soon."

Soon he found a straight up cliff wall north of where he was riding. Billy Joe headed for it thinking, 'I can always hunker down on the south side of that wall and at least get out of the wind that's driving this hail.'

Visibility was dropping fast, making it harder to see more than a few feet in front of them. As they approached the wall they were sheltered somewhat from the wind and the sting of the hail stones. The horse suddenly turned left and started walking along the face of the cliff. Why did B.J. turn this way? He is from wild horse stock so I trust him.

They rounded an out cropping of rock and a large black hole in the wall yawned open in front of them. "B.J. you did it, you found us shelter." The cave was large enough that he led the horse in with him.

Scouting around Billy Joe found a packrat's nest. "This is perfect for starting a fire." Soon he had a fire going.

"B.J., I'm going to go out there and find us some fuel for the fire, that packrats nest won't last long and the way the temperature is dropping I suspect we are going to be in for a long cold night. I'm going to leave the saddle on you it will help keep you warm."

As he stepped out of the cave the sleet and hail had turned to snow. Large flakes were being driven by the wind. The effect was snow blowing sideways created a white out condition. If I get out there and get turned around and can't find my way back to this cave, I will die.

Billy Joe went back and took the lariat rope off his saddle and tied one end of it to a knurled cedar growing out of the rock near the entrance. I hope I can find fuel within the length of this rope. He tied the other end of the rope around his waist.

He walked about ten steps when his toe struck something below the snow. Billy Joe reached down and found a large branch that wind had dropped on the ground at some time or other. When he picked it up, it was about twelve feet long. This will last a little while, I'll drag it in and come back to see what else I can find.

It took only a few minutes for him to chop the limb into sections and place two sections on the flames. The cave started to warm. Billy Joe knew that small pile of logs would not keep the fire going all night.

"B.J. I brought in the first log it's your turn to go out in that cold and get some more." The horse rolled his eyes and looked at Billy Joe and snorted.

"Alright big mouth. I'll go back out there. I'm going to figure out a way to teach you to bring in the wood." B.J. shoved Billy Joe with his nose toward the opening.

"You don't have to be so pushy. I'm going." This time he angled to the left as he walked out the entrance. He was almost to the end of the rope when he found a large branch that had split off the trunk but was still attached. Using his bowie knife he cut it free and dragged it to the cave. Using his hatchet, he soon had this limb cut into usable sections.

"I'm going to stop and make some coffee, and warm up a little before I go back out there." Opening a saddlebag he took out a bag of corn and poured it into his hat. Then he slipped the bridle off B.J. so the horse could eat the corn more comfortably.

Sitting there in the cave holding a metal cup full of steaming coffee. He could hear that the wind was picking up and looking out he could not see beyond the entrance. Looking back at the pile of fuel, "I wonder if that will hold until the wind dies down. I do not want to venture out in that storm."

'I wonder if anyone will ever find my body if I don't make it through the night? There are hundreds of men who disappear in this country and are never heard from again.' Sitting there alone in a cold damp cave a young man felt so alone. *I wonder what mom and dad are doing tonight. What are my sisters doing tonight? They may be getting ready for a dance.*

Then his thoughts turned to Mary Beth. Chills ran through him that were not caused by the storm. "B.J. we've got to get out of here in the morning, Mary Beth may be in trouble. They are north west of here, the storm would have hit them before it got here. I hope they are okay. What about the outlaws that are kidnaping women and girls?" He felt fear creeping into his bones. He was trapped, he couldn't get to Mary Beth to protect her. "Her dad is a good man, but he can't stand against those outlaws."

Billy Joe bowed his head and said, "Oh Lord, I desperately need your help. Please protect Mary Beth and her dad until I can get there." Then he vowed that he would survive this storm and as soon as he and B.J. could move they would go directly to Mary Beth's home. Then the fear returned, what if I am too late?

CHAPTER THIRTY-SIX

S ix men gathered around the potbellied stove in the store for a meeting. Miles Cafton, stood and said, "Gentlemen we are all gathered here because we have a problem."

One of the others said, "You can say that again, we have a problem."

"Yeah, we came here to build homes for our families. Instead we are starving. We don't have material to build houses. Most of us are living in sod houses or dug outs. Hell the Indians are living better."

"There are so many people here there is no game left to hunt." Another man said.

"My crop got destroyed by the hail storm."

"I had a good crop but six masked men robbed me and took it before I could get home with the money. I busted my hump working in the hot boiling sun for nothing. Six thugs with guns just rode up and took it."

"Now those same, or I assume it's the same, men are going to people's homes and telling them that they will protect the farmers but the farmer must agree to give them fifty percent of next year's crop as their fee for protecting the farmer. I swear it's the same guys who are robbing farmers this year that are now demanding that we agree to give them half of each year to protect us from robbers."

"Basically we have become share croppers on our own land."

"We were better off back home where at least the landlord gave us a house to live in."

"Gentlemen we have got to form a government, we need to elect us a sheriff, we need to form some townships. Right now we are one hundred thousand people scattered over three hundred square miles." Miles Caftan said. "I have sent a petition to Washington asking them to send Federal Marshals to bring law and order to this area until we can elect peace officers. I have also asked that loans to purchase building materials be made available to us. We are not asking for a handout just a loan until we can get a crop in and sold then we can and will gladly repay the loans. Let me see a show of hands, how many could use a loan and would be willing to repay it when you get your crops in next year."

"Yeah but what about that bunch of thugs that are demanding that we give them half of the crop each year?"

"If we could get a good man elected sheriff in each section of this settlement, how many would be willing to give ten-percent of your crop to pay his salary and for any deputies he might hire?"

"If he could get rid of those thugs that are demanding fifty-percent, ten- percent is a lot better than fifty."

"If we can find a good man who was willing to do the job, how many of you would pledge to support him and his deputies?"

"Who determined where the county lines were to be?"

"The government surveyors."

"We have a provisional government set up in Stillwater," the lawyer said, "I'm going to ride over there and see what I can find out about getting us some help."

"Can we name our county, right now they are all just numbered?"

"I don't know. I could offer a name for our county to them in Stillwater when I go over there."

"I don't want to be just called number four any more. You know where I came from all the counties were named after famous people, I lived in Jefferson county."

"Come to think of it we lived in Toole county named after the first settler."

"I'll ask them and if they say we can, we can all put up a name for the county and everybody can vote on it. I like that." He pulled out his pocket watch and said, "Okay, let's meet here one month from today. Hopefully I will have received an answer from Washington by then, each one of you think about what name you want on your county and who you know that might consider the job of sheriff and bring both names to the next meeting. Winter is coming on so there is not much we can do except hunker down until spring gets here anyway. I want us to get organized and have a plan in place before our crops come in next fall."

One of the other men said, "If we can find a good man to take the job of sheriff, he better be pretty good with a six-gun, because those outlaws are pretty mean fellows. They won't scare off very easy."

"What about that young man who runs the sawmill, didn't some of you talk to him?"

"Yes when we talked to him he wasn't interested. I went out to his place this week but he wasn't there. I left a card and asked him to come see me."

"I understand he's hell on wheels with a six-gun but level headed for a young man."

"Yeah, and he ain't married so he has no family to worry about."

CHAPTER THIRTY-SEVEN

It was noon the next day when Billy Joe got the tree chopped up and the fire wood stacked in the cave. Chewing on some hard tack he said, "B.J. I hope you are ready to cover some snow covered ground. I think we have a day and a half's ride to get to Mary Beth and her dad, but I don't want to spend another night on the trail so I want to keep going until we get there. You better not go lame on me or throw a shoe. I might just take off and leave you on your own, I am that excited to see Mary Beth."

The horse twitched his ears and snorted.

When Billy Joe led B.J. out of the cave and climbed into the saddle, it wasn't snowing but it was cold, "B.J. I'm guessing it must be between ten and fifteen degrees. At least the wind is not blowing. Those clouds sure look like they could dump some more snow on us. I think Chippewa Creek is West of us. We go West until we hit the creek and follow it North West to find their place."

Every slow painful cold mile Billy Joe could feel his anxiety growing, "B.J., I wish you had wings so we could fly on over there and make sure they're alright. I just have a bad feeling we need to get there as fast as we can."

If it weren't for the feeling of urgency he would have enjoyed the scene before him, The whole world was blanketed in a beautiful white blanket, the air was pure and clean, the silence was sweet to his ears. The only sound was the soft squish of the horse's hooves in the new fallen snow.

"B.J., I would love to take time to enjoy this scenery, but we have to move fast. I don't know why but I just have a feeling that we need to hurry."

He leaned down and patted the horses' neck. Coming to the creek Billy Joe turned North West to follow the creek as it flowed between two hills. On the other side of the creek about a quarter of a mile in front of him, he spotted a cabin in the trees. There was smoke curling up from the chimney.

Approaching the cabin Billy Joe called out, "Hello the cabin."

A young woman in a thread bare cotton dress opened the door and looked out. Looking closer Billy Joe could see two little heads peeping around their mother.

"Sir are you just traveling through."

"Yes ma'am."

"Sir can you help us?"

"Ma'am I'm traveling light, all I 've got with me is a little coffee and some hard tack you are sure welcome to that. Where is your husband?"

"He took our crop to sell and never came back. He must be dead."

"I am sorry I don't have more, but I am in a hurry to get to see about my fiancé. Maybe I can stop by on my way back and see what I can do."

"Sir please don't forget about us, we're desperate. All of the food is gone. This provision you gave us will help a little but not long."

CHAPTER THIRTY-EIGHT

S nake walked into the bank with two canvas bags full of gold coins and some US script. He had stopped by the haberdasher shop and purchased a new black suit with fine red threads woven in to form thin textured stripes. His brand new black boots gleamed, his six-gun was out of sight behind his vest.

A man in a white shirt and bow tie greeted him, "Yes sir, I am Philip, how can I help you?"

At least he is not staring at my scar. "Well I would like to open an account, and I need a reference to a good person to purchase property from."

"Sir I will be happy to assist you in opening a new account. Do you have a deposit you wish to make today?"

Snake simply pointed to the two canvas bags he was holding in his left hand.

"I can take care of that for you sir. What name should be on the account? "

"My name of course."

"Sir you haven't told me your name."

"Oh pardon my manners, I'm Jake Calvert. I just moved here from the gold fields in Colorado Territory. As you can see, I have been quite successful in my mining operations."

When they had the account open and the money safely deposited, Jake said, "Now I would like to purchase a nice place to live and possibly get married and settle down here in Oklahoma City. I believe this city offers a great potential for future investments,"

"Oh, it most certainly does." Phillip said, "As to the real-estate. What type of real-estate investment are you seeking?"

"A home for a gentleman and his family."

"I might have just the home you are looking for. We have a customer that is recently widowed, and I believe she is interested in selling her home. She wants to move back to Ohio where her family is. Would you like for me to arrange a meeting between the two of you?"

"Is it a nice home?"

"Very nice. I suspect that it is a property a gentleman like yourself would enjoy owning. If I contact her and she is agreeable to meet with you, how can I reach you later today?"

"I'll be staying at the Peabody until a home can be purchased. "

"Very well I'll send a runner to ask for an appointment for you to tour the home and visit with the owner. As soon as he returns I'll send him to find you. If you like we can handle the transfer of title for you."

Snake pulled an expensive cigar out of his pocket as soon as he walked out of the bank. *All I have to do is keep those hay seeds paying me half their crops and I can live like a king. Maybe I'll even run for Governor when this becomes a state. As long as I can keep a rein on the gang and keep them out at Yoder's place, collecting my share of every crop sold, I can live like a king.*

The best thing I did was make Knowles the straw boss of that bunch. I told him to make sure none of them came into Oklahoma City to blow off steam. It would be bad if they did. As soon as I get all of those lily livered farmers to sign over their deeds to me, I'll get rid of almost all of those thugs and hire me a real farm manager to run the whole operation. Nothing is going to stop me now, I'll kill anyone who gets in the way. In fact, I still have a score to settle with Sam McClanton back down in Texas for whipping me like a dog with a horse whip.

Then Snake thought about old man Carpenter's daughter, *now that is a classy woman, she would make a proper wife for a gentleman like I'm going to be. I think I'll just stop by and make a call on them on my way back to Yoder's place. If I had her by my side, people would be looking at her instead of this hideous scar. I'm still gonna kill that dude for this scar.*

CHAPTER THIRTY-NINE

Mary Beth touched her pa's brow and it was red hot. She bowed her head and said, **Holy Father, please show me what to do to help my dad. I am so lost I have no idea what to do. I wish Billy Joe was here. Please send someone to help me. I don't want to watch my daddy die because I didn't know what to do to help him.**

She jumped and whirled around. Somebody had knocked on her door. She breathed a thank you for sending somebody to help. Let it be Billy Joe.

When she opened the door a well-dressed man with a horrible scar on his face stood there with his hat in his hands. Except for the scar, he looked like a gentleman.

Before she could say anything he said, "Good afternoon, my name is Jake Calvert I am your neighbor, I farm a place just South West of here? Can I come in and talk with you and your husband for a minute."

"Mr. Calvert, I live with my father and right now he is very sick. I'm sorry, I know he would love to meet you, but right now he is down with a high fever."

"Do you have any medicine to give him?"

"No."

"How long has he had a fever?"

"Three days."

"Make sure he drinks plenty of water. Don't let him get dehydrated. I'll come back and bring something to help break his fever."

"Oh, thank you sir. I was just praying for God to send someone to help me. He sent you."

Snake stuck his hat back on and said, "Sometimes things work in mysterious ways." With that he touched his hat brim and mounted his horse. "Don't be afraid, get him to drink some water. I'll be back soon."

CHAPTER FORTY

Billy Joe knew he couldn't push B.J. any faster. When he left the cave this morning he thought it was probably about thirty miles to Mary Beth's father's farm he knew it would be a long hard ride to get there in one day. When he left the cave this morning, the need to hurry was heavy on him, cover any tracks he couldn't stand the thought of not getting there tonight. "B.J., I know you're struggling, these snow drifts are deep. I'll bet we haven't covered ten miles today and it's going to be dark soon. Plus, those clouds look like they could dump a lot more snow on us. As bad as I hate too, we're going to have to find another place to camp tonight."

Riding toward the cliff he looked for a cave. None appeared, it was getting darker and colder, the snow had started falling again. "B.J., we're going to be in big trouble if I don't find shelter soon."

＝╪ ╪＝

Snake rode into Yoder's place, and put his horse in the barn. Carrying his rifle in his left hand with his saddle bags over his left shoulder he stepped through the back door.

"Yoder, do you have medicine here for fever?"

"Do you have a fever?"

"No not me. That man that lives on the place East of here, I stopped by there and talked to his daughter she said he had a fever for the last three days."

Yoder walked over to a shelf and took down a small canvas bag. Handing it to Snake he said, "Take this to them. Tell the lady this is willow bark. She should boil some bark in water and when it cools enough get her father to drink it."

"What is this some voo-doo junk?"

"No, the Indians use it all the time to break a fever."

Snake decided it was too late to go back tonight but he would go first thing in the morning.

CHAPTER FORTY-ONE

B illy Joe found two large cedar trees growing together against the face of the rock wall. Riding up to the cedars he stepped down from the saddle. Stiff and cold as he was he knew he had to get himself and B.J. some shelter or they could both be dead before morning.

He took out his razor sharp Bowie knife and started cutting branches from the bottom of both trees. Snow was packed on to the outer limbs. As he tunneled into the lower branches the trees became like an igloo. Working into the base of the cedar trees he widened the space by cutting more branches out of the back side nearest the cliff wall.

Soon he could stand up in the hollowed-out space. Leading B.J. into the hollowed-out space he took branches that he had cut out and stacked them into the opening. The falling snow soon covered the opening into the base of the two trees.

Up against the rock wall the snow was not as thick as it was on the area away from the cliff. Taking some of the cut branches he started a small fire against the wall. He pulled his coffee pot from his saddle bag and shook some coffee grounds into it. Soon, with a tin cup full of steaming hot horse shoe coffee, he started to thaw out. "B.J., I wish we had something to eat, it's actually not too bad in here."

Finding a comfortable way to sleep turned out to be difficult. The cedar leaves were really scratchy, making it nearly impossible to get comfortable. Sometime during the night, the wind died down then Billy Joe heard wolves sniffing around the cedar trees. *They smell BJ in here.* He shivered when he thought what would happen to him if he lost his horse.

It was just getting light when Snake rode back into the yard at the Carpenter place. "Hello the house." He called from fifty feet away. He knew nobody in his right mind rode up to a house without any warning, that was good way to get shot right out of the saddle.

Then he stepped down and walked to the door. When he knocked Mary Beth called out from inside, "Who is it"

"Jake Calvert. I brought some medicine."

He heard the bar being removed from across the door. As he stepped in he also noticed she was holding a large forty-four in her right hand.

"No offence Mr. Calvert, but I don't know you. I appreciate you bringing something to help my father."

"I don't blame you for being careful. There are some outlaws around. You won't need that with me. I need a cooking pot to fill with water so we can boil this willow bark. The Indians claim when the water is cool we get your father to drink this and it will break his fever."

Mary Beth looked at him for a moment then walked over to the cabinet and laid the gun down.

Soon they had the pieces of willow bark steeping on the hearth of the fire place. Mary Beth said, "Mr. Calvert, I appreciate what you've done for my father. I had nothing to give him, all I could do was keep cool wet rags on his brow."

"I would never leave a lady as beautiful as you in distress. Let's get the old man to drink this willow bark broth." As soon as Mr. Carpenter had drank the broth, Snake said, "We need to get him well, a pretty little thing like you doesn't need to be wasting away taking care of an old man."

"Sir, I beg your pardon. You are talking about my father. He is not just some old man."

"Oh you are feisty and pretty I like that. Honey I aim to take you away from this dirt and grime out here on the prairie. I have a new home in the city and you'll love the lights, music and dancing. We'll dress you in the finest and your beauty will be on display for all to see."

"Of all the gall. You ride in here offering to help my father and then you start talking like that. I have no intention of going any-where with you."

"You know I could just throw you over my saddle and take you with me."

A cold voice behind him said, "You wouldn't get far with six forty-four slugs in your belly."

Snake whipped around and Billy Joe stood there with a six gun in his right hand. "You are buttin' in on something that ain't none of your business."

"Snake, when I hear you tell my girl you can throw her over your saddle and take her with you that makes it my business."

Snake eyed Billy Joe, oh he wanted to draw so bad but one look in the young man's eyes told him he would never make it. "Who did you say you was?"

"Billy Joe McClanton."

"I remember you, you're one of the McClanton's from down in Texas." He touched the side of his face. "I'm gonna kill you for this. If you didn't have the drop on me I'd kill you with my bare hands."

Billy Joe calmly dropped the six-shooter back into the holster.

CHAPTER FORTY-TWO

When he dropped his gun back into the holster he was ready in case Snake went for his six-shooter. Instead Snake roared like a wounded buffalo and charged across the room with the intent to maim that brass young man.

Billy Joe's arms and shoulders were rock hard from swinging that big double bladed ax for the past year. Billy Joe calmly stepped to meet him and shot a rock hard left into Snake's face. Cutting a gash under his right eye.

Snake was surprised and stunned, but when he reached up and touched his face and his hand came back bloody he went berserk. Screaming at the top of his lungs, swinging both fists as fast as he could he charged again. This time there were too many blows for Billy Joe to dodge them all. A clubbing right fist caught him over the left eye causing a red stream to cloud his vision in that eye.

Both fighters were toe to toe slugging it out when the unmistakable sound of a six-shooter's hammer being cocked filled the room.

"Mr. Calvert, or whoever you are, you have ten seconds to get out of my house before I blow you away."

Both fighters looked and Mary Beth stood there holding a cocked and loaded forty-four. she said, "One, two."

"Snake Calvert, looked at her then turned to Billy Joe and said, "This ain't over. I'll catch you when she is not around to defend you."

"Mr. if you as much as speak to this lady again I will hunt you down like I would a mad dog. Now get out of this house before she does shoot you."

Snake stormed out the door slamming it behind him. As soon as the door slammed Mary Beth was in Billy Joe's arms. "Oh Billy Joe, I've been praying that you would come."

"I would have been here two days ago but the storm stopped me. I know that man, he runs with a bunch of renegades. What was he doing here?"

"My dad has been really sick. He has had a fever for three days. I had no medicine to give him. I was wishing you were here. Then yesterday afternoon that man stopped in and said he was a neighbor. I told him my father was real sick with a fever and he offered to come back with some medicine. Instead he showed up with some pieces of willow bark and had me boil them then get daddy to drink the broth. He said the Indians used it to break the fever."

"Well he was right about that, the willow bark is good medicine. Did you give some to your pa?"

"Yes, we had just finished getting pa to drink the broth when he started saying crazy things. He scared me," She shivered thinking about it. "Thank God you got here when you did."

"When I came up to knock on the door, I saw a strange horse outside, then I heard your voice and you sounded up-set so I pushed the door open instead of knocking. He was so busy running off his mouth he never heard the door open."

She picked up a clean cloth off the counter and wiped the blood from his brow. "Why did you put your gun back in the holster and give him a chance to hit you?"

"Because somebody needed to teach him some manners. His mama sure didn't"

"But you could've gotten hurt bad."

"Didn't happen though did it. How's your pa?"

They walked into the other room, Mr. Carpenter was sleeping, his breathing was steady and strong. Mary Beth touched is brow and said, "His fever is gone."

"The bark from a willow tree has a product called aspirin in it and it often knocks out fever very quickly. Now I hope you have some more because the fever may come back and we'll need to give him some more."

"Yes, he left a bag of bark pieces here. Billy Joe, the man was rude and uncouth, he had an ugly scar on his face, but he saved daddy's life. Now do I hate him for being rude or love him for saving my dad?"

"Our pastor used to always say, hate the sin, love the sinner. In this case I think we can love the kind act and dislike the sinner."

CHAPTER FORTY-THREE

S nake stormed into Yoder's house and snatched up a whiskey bottle and took a big swig. "Listen up, we've gotta make some plans. We are gonna do two raids, first I found out that the army is sending the payroll next week for the fort. They will be carrying over twenty-thousand dollars. I know where we can hit them and get away clean. Second I just saw that worthless no count McClanton kid over at the Carpenter place."

"Where is the Carpenter place?'

"You know where we saw that pretty woman hanging wash on the line."

"If you saw him why didn't you kill'em?

"Because I was talking to the woman and he snuck up behind me and had a gun on me before I knew he was anywhere around. I told him, you've got the drop on me now but the next time I see you I'm gonna kill ya. After I kill him I want to ride down to Texas and kill his pa. We might even take those pretty little uppity sisters of his and make a run to Mexico with'em. If we have that army payroll we can live like kings down in Mexico."

⊷⊶ ⊷⊶

The next morning Mr. Carpenter's condition had improved, his color was better and he sat up eating some cornmeal mush and drinking some coffee,.

"Mary Beth, I met a young woman not much older than you who had three babes in the cabin with her and they were out of food. I gave her the pack I had with me which wasn't much since I had to spend two extra nights getting here."

"Where was she?"

"About an hour Southeast of here"

"What was her name?"

"I don't know. I didn't even ask her."

"Wait until tomorrow morning, if pa is still doing well I'll ride with you and we'll go see what we can do for them."

"Mary Beth if she doesn't have anything to feed those babies she can't wait until tomorrow. She needs help now."

"I guess you are right. Let me pack some food for you to take with you."

"Let me borrow an ax, to take with me, so when I get there, I can chop some wood for her too."

About an hour later Billy Joe topped a ridge and spotted a big buck deer about one hundred yards down the other side. Instinctively he whipped out his Winchester and put a shot right through the deer's neck. "Okay B.J. let's go dress out that deer. I'll take the meat with me, I'm sure that lady and her babies can use some more meat, at least as cold as it is the meat will not spoil very quickly. I'll hang it up so the critters can't get at it."

Billy Joe approached the cabin leading a pack horse filled with fresh meat and food supplies. Stopping the horse, some ways off he said, "B.J. something's wrong. I don't see any smoke coming out of that chimney."

Billy Joe slipped the Winchester out of his saddle scabbard and rode cautiously toward the cabin. He studied the ground as he rode, it was covered in fresh horse tracks. "Whoa, wait a minute, I don't recognize any of those tracks. For -sure, none of those tracks were made by the horse Snake has been riding, I know cause, I memorized them."

As Billy Joe got down off his horse he studied the horse tracks on the ground. "Those tracks were not made by Snakes group. I know those tracks. I wonder who they were?"

Holding his Winchester in his right hand he slowly pushed to door open without knocking. When he stepped up on the stoop he could see the place had been ransacked. The table was turned over; the chairs were scattered about, the mattress was off the bed. "Somebody was looking for something. I wonder where the woman and babies are?"

Stepping back outside a robber jay hopped from limb to limb screeching at him. Other than that it was deathly quiet, as if all of nature was holding its breath. "Did they take the lady and kids with them? What were they looking for?"

Walking out a little farther he studied the horse tracks with care. He stood up and looked all around. "By the looks of these tracks they didn't take her with them none of the tracks are deeper going out than they were coming in. Where can she be?"

He stood listening for any sound, sniffing the air like a wild animal for any unusual smell, nothing. He then walked around behind the cabin. He pushed his Stetson back on his head, "I'll be darn look at that I see three tracks leading out into the woods she must be carrying the baby and leading the older ones. Maybe I can follow her tracks. Then again I might lead those guys right to her and the kids if they come back and see my tracks too."

He stood there thinking for several minutes, *what should I do?* "She's probably hiding out and watching the cabin. So when she doesn't see anybody for a while she can come back. I think I'll unload the pack horse and leave the supplies so when she does get back she can feed the kids."

He busied himself straightening up the cabin and unloading the supplies. Then thought, she doesn't have a gun. "I've got a spare six-shooter in my saddle bag. I'll leave it and a box of shells. That way if they do come back she might be able to stand them off."

As he mounted up it started to snow." Well, B.J. that might be a good thing the snow will cover any tracks she left. I just hope she found a cave or some good shelter. If she didn't, she better hurry back to this cabin pretty soon they could freeze out there. Maybe I should stay here until they get back, I could go in and get a fire going so the cabin will be warm. If those guys do come back I could make them feel mighty unwelcome." He climbed back down and went back into the cabin.

"There's plenty of wood stacked in the log rack for now. First I'll get a fire going and warm the place up then I'll get busy and straighten the place up. They sure made a mess of things whoever those jaspers were."

Half an hour later Billy Joe had a roaring fire going, the chill was out of the room, the furniture, such as it was, was straightened up, the bed was made up and he had a pot of cowboy coffee on. "Now all I need to do is sit down and wait. Maybe I orta cut off a couple of them venison steaks and start them to roasting. That lady and those babies are probably gonna be hungry when they do get back. In fact if she smells steaks roasting she might hurry back. Come to think of it, the babies probably can't eat steaks. I'll unpack all of those supplies that Mary Beth sent 'em. It'll have something the little ones can eat."

Billy Joe's stomach started to growl when he smelled the steaks roasting. "Well I have two on the spit and she can't eat both of 'em so I'll eat one. I guess I should wait until they get here but since I don't know when they are coming, I think I'll go ahead and eat one of those steaks now."

Grabbing a tin plate, he plopped one of the venison steaks down on it and added some beans he had in the pot. Slicing off a chunk of sour dough bread and with a cup of cowboy coffee he had a feast in front of him.

After he had eaten he wiped out his plate and sat down with a cup of coffee to wait. The wind made a mournful sound around the eaves of the cabin. His ears strained to hear the sound of that lady and those babies coming. He felt so useless just sitting there, but he couldn't think of anything else he could do. He had no way of knowing where she and the babies might be. He bowed his head and prayed, *"Lord I know I don't talk to you enough, I know you are kinda busy so I don't bother you too much but I need your help tonight, somewhere out there in the cold dark night there is a young mother with three little babies she needs you really bad. Please help her, can you send one of them angels to watch over them. I'll keep the fire going so the cabin will be warm if you could just lead them back home. Amen."*

The hours seemed to drag by, every sound seemed to be magnified, he was straining so hard to hear them approaching the cabin. All he heard was the cold wind and the occasional crack of a tree branch breaking off in the wind. He knew it was a terrible night for a young mother and those babies to be out in the cold. Then he wondered who were the riders and what were they after, she certainly didn't appear to have anything they could steal.

Slowly fatigue over took him and his eyes slowly closed and his head slumped down on the table in front of him.

CHAPTER FORTY-FOUR

A large wagon pulled up in front of the saw mill.

Jacob stepped out, "Yes sir, what can I do for ya?"

"Y'all still got some lumber to sell?'

"Yes sir sure do. What 'cha lookin' for?"

"I need a hundred of them 2 by 6s and a hundred 1 by 6s."

"Pull your wagon on around here and we'll get'er loaded for ya. How far did ya come?"

The man pointed West and said, "I come a pretty fer piece took me two days to get here. I figure it'll take three to get back with a load on."

"How are things over in your neck of the woods?"

"Well I never heard it called that, there sure ain't no woods over that way just a few Mesquite trees but I know what cha mean. Things are pretty bad. There have been several robberies and killings over that away." He reached down and patted his holster and said, "That is why I don't go to the outhouse unless I got ole Bessie here with me. How about around here?'

"It's been pretty quiet. We have been hearing about a lot going on Northwest of here. You never know when that'll change."

"They have got to get us a sheriff or a marshal or get the army back in here or something."

"Well I heard the other day about two guys who were arguing over which side of the creek was the property line and one of 'em pulled out a gun and killed the other one. The way I hear it the man who got killed had a wife and three little babies. I worry about my daughter and her family they got a place up North of here."

"You are right, something has got to be done. You're all loaded up and here is your receipt. Be careful going back."

As the wagon was rolling away three more wagons rolled up in a cloud of dust. Jacob's first thought was, 'they must need a lot of lumber.' Then he noticed that all of the wagons had at least two men with rifles.

"You fellows are traveling pretty heavy loaded with guns."

"Pardner it is getting pretty bad out there. We all needed lumber so we decided to come together. Better chance of getting through. We had three neighbors shot down in the last week."

"Y'all climb down, I've got a pot of coffee on, get 'cha a slug of it then you can tell me what you need."

As they drank coffee the men told of lawlessness everywhere. Thugs were sitting back waiting for a man to build a house and barns then shooting him down and taking over. Each of these men owned property that joined. They were going to build their houses at the junction of the four pieces of land. That way they would be close enough that they could defend each other.

"Sounds like you are building a village."

"No sir each one of us owns a section of land and rather than build our houses one mile apart we are going to build at the corners where all four sections of land meet. Each man's house will be on his six-hundred and forty acres. We'll just be within rifle shot of each other if those dudes try to move in."

"Do you know who they are?'

"The Thornton gang started it, now we are hearing that there are several that are copying their style."

"It's gettin' bad out there. If I'd knowed it was gonna be like this, I would have stayed in Tennessee. Somebody has got to do something. We are each trying to protect our own."

When the wagons were loaded each man counted out the money he owed. One of them said, "Young fella y'all better be careful here because if they find out your collecting cash money. You can bet they'll come after you."

One of the others said, "Yeah it won't take long. If they see three wagons comin' back loaded with new boards, they are gonna know somebody was selling 'em."

———

Mary Beth sat down in front of the fire place and opened her Bible. It opened to 2nd Samuel. As she read she came to verse three.

My God, my rock, in whom I take refuge, My shield and the horn of my salvation, my stronghold and my refuge; My savior, You save me from violence.

She looked at that verse then she noticed that there was a tiny little reference note beside it that told her this same subject was also in Psalms 18:2 - Turning to that verse it read, "*The LORD is my rock and my fortress and my deliverer, My God, my rock, in whom I take refuge; My shield and the horn of my salvation, my stronghold.*"

She closed her Bible and Prayed, "*Oh Lord I know you led me to those two verses. You know I am afraid, yet you reminded me that you are my protector. Lord I pray that your protection will also cover Billy Joe and the young mother with the small kids. Father as you know there are evil men all around us we need your protection now more than ever before. Father I thank you for the improvement in my Daddy and I thank you for Billy Joe, for he is a good and strong man, the kind we need in these times. I pray that you will protect him and bring him back safe to me. Father I pray for that young mother and her babies, I pray that you will send an angel to watch over her tonight. Amen."*

———◄╬╬► ———

It was growing dark and getting colder as the young mother and the three babies huddled in the back of a cave. She had taken the kids to look for some berries or nuts. so she could feed them something. She had only walked a little way into the forest when she heard horses coming to the cabin. Thinking her husband had returned she started back but when she could see the cabin she realized that it was not her husband. Hiding below the low hanging branches of a cedar tree she watched. "Kids be real quiet until mommy figures out what is going on."

She could hear a lot of cussing and fussing and she could hear the cabin being torn apart. "I wonder what they want. We sure don't have anything they can steal?"

She eased back out from under the cedar tree and moved away from the cabin deeper into the trees. After about an hour of walking she found a cave, just as she and the babies got inside the cave it started snowing.

She huddled in the back of the cold dark cave wishing she had matches so she could gather up some kindling and start a fire. She thought about her husband, "I know he's dead. Because by now he would be back. It's been four days since I last saw him. He was going to work clearing some brush along that creek on the west side of our property. I don't know whether some claim jumpers got him or some renegade Indians, but I just know he's dead. Thornton L. Craddick was a good man, a good husband and a good father."

The baby started to whimper, "Mommy I cold."

She cuddled the baby to her breast to try to share some of her warmth, then reaching over with her right arm she pulled the other two little girls close to her side. She had never felt so scared and alone in her whole life. The wind moaned in the mouth of the cave.

She didn't know what else to do so she started to pray. "*Oh God if you are really up there, my name is Elisabeth Thornton, please don't let my babies die in this dark cold cave. God, all I ask is for you to protect them until it is daylight again so I can find my way back to the cabin where I can get them inside and build a fire. God I still don't have any food to feed them, is it asking too much for you to help me find something I can feed the precious little ones too?*"

Fumbling around in the dark cave she felt a pack rat nests. "If I had a match I could get a fire going with the material from that nest." Feeling around some more she found two large chunks of rock. "Lord help me to make a spark between these two rocks big enough to get a little fire going for my babies." She struck the rocks together and a small spark flew off the rocks but it went out before it struck the material from the nest.

Her hands were cold, she dropped one of the rocks. Fumbling around she found the second rock and tried again to strike them together with enough force to cause a large spark. She was so tired and hungry herself, what if she didn't have enough strength to get the fire started. The baby started to cry softly.

She took her hands and piled the nest material up more, then with her last ounce of strength she grabbed both rocks and slammed them together in the dark cave. A large shower of sparks rained down on the nest material and a small flame started. Bending down she gently blew on the small flame until it grew into a real flame. "Praise God, I have a small fire. A small fire in a cave can keep us from freezing to death. Oh Lord, in the morning help me find something the feed the babies. Lord you led us to shelter and provided us with a fire to keep the cold off, please watch over us the rest of this night."

"My pa always told me to make your fire next to the wall and sit facing the wall, that way the rock wall will reflect the heat back to you." The fire was small, but it gave off enough light that she could see other pack rat nests and she knew she had to use the material sparingly if she wanted it to last until morning. She pulled the girls close to her and sat with her back to the entrance of the cave and faced the warmth of the fire reflecting off the rocks forming the back wall. As they warmed, the babies fell asleep, soon she was nodding too, out of sheer exhaustion and hunger.

CHAPTER FORTY-FIVE

Billy Joe woke with a start, the first thing he noticed was that the fire had burned down to just embers. Quickly he jumped up and grabbed some logs to add to the embers. Then he noticed the sound. It was quiet, the wind had calmed down. He walked over and opened the door and saw moon light reflecting on the white snow. He knew the first snow was usually a deep one so there was no chance of finding the woman's tracks now. "I just hope they found a warm shelter."

Billy Joe got busy and put a pot of coffee on to brew. "I'll wait until day light and fry up a batch of bacon, maybe the smell of bacon will lead her back to the cabin."

Billy Joe took out his guns and one by one cleaned and reloaded them, while drinking the strong black coffee. "If those jaspers come back here today I may need these guns. "

※

Elizabeth heard something above the moan of the wind. "Somebody is coming." At first she was glad, then she thought, *what if it's the bad guys.*

The sounds of something or someone was coming closer. She tried to shrink back farther into a small knot with the babies.

Snow fell from the bush out side of the cave as if something or someone had brushed against it. Elizabeth looked around in the dark cave for a stick or even a large rock, anything she could use as a weapon. "It can't be anybody coming to rescue us because I don't know a soul out here."

The wind even seemed to lose its power. She said, "The clouds must be moving away, when I look around, I can see the moonlight glistening on the white snow."

Then it happened. Her tired brain refused to accept what her eyes were telling her. A giant grizzly bear had lumbered into the cave. It sniffed the air then reared up on its hind legs and roared. The most terrifying sound she had ever heard. It was a monster, its head touched the top of the cave. It dropped down on all four feet and moved a few feet into the cave and reared up again sniffing the air, then bellowed a roar that made the rock walls seem to vibrate. She screamed, "Oh God help me."

Turning her back to the bear she grabbed the three babies and clutched them to her breast. An old Indian man reached over her left shoulder and poked a long spear into the fire. The end of the spear spring into flames. The Indian pulled it back, then she heard the bear make a funny whining sound. She was terrified to look around but she had to know what was going on. Turning she saw the old Indian standing between her and the bear. He pushed the burning end of the spear into the bear's face.

The beast snorted and shook his head from side to side. The old Indian pulled back the spear then pushed it back under the bear's chin.

Turning her back to the giant bear she scooped the girls even tighter into her arms as if her frail body could protect them from a thousand pound angry, hungry bear and an Indian.

It took a moment for her brain to register what was happening in the cave. The bear making angry, frightened noises was moving out of the cave not coming closer. The old Indian was yelling something in a language that she had never heard before. Then it was quiet. Terror held her frozen in place, she couldn't move her arms or legs, she felt paralyzed. Was she losing her mind too? Did she actually see a bear come into the cave? Where could the Indian have come from? Was there an actual Indian that saved them? Was she hallucinating because of hunger and cold? Then her three year old daughter said, "Mommy, where did he go?"

"Who baby?"

"The man who chased off the bear."

"Did you see a man and a bear?"

"Yes mommy, he was a big mean looking bear then the man stuck a stick in our fire and got it on fire and chased the bear out of the cave."

Elizabeth started to cry, tears streamed down her face. "Don't cry mommy, that man won't let the bear come back."

Billy Joe's first thought was where can they be? I better get the fire rekindled surely they will come back as soon as it is daylight. Then he said, "What if those men come back instead?" He reached down and checked the loads in his guns.

He got busy and rekindled the fire then put water on to make coffee. The stuffed he had fixed for supper was still on the edge of the fire, by now it was cold. "Should I warm that up or throw it out and fix something fresh for them? "

The venison steaks didn't look too appetizing, they were all shriveled up and black. The biscuits were hard as rocks, Picking it all up he walked to the door and threw it out in the snow, "Let the critters eat it."

He then put on a pan of water to get hot, "I'll mix in some oat meal for the little ones and I'll make some new biscuits and fry some fresh bacon, then use the grease to make some gravy. Maybe by the time that is done the lady and those babies will come in."

He sat down sipping on some coffee and his stomach started to growl so he picked up a biscuit and a piece of bacon and started munching on it.

By midmorning Billy Joe said, "Well I'll leave the fire banked and water in the pan, so if she does get back she can feed the babies. I'd go out and look for her but I have no idea which way to start, so I guess I better ride on back and tell Mary Beth what is going on then I need to get back to the sawmill."

CHAPTER FORTY-SIX

Jon Yoder came in from the fields to find Snake and all his men gone except the youngest one they called Slim. "Where are the others?"

"The boss heard about a train carrying an army payroll coming through Kansas, so they are gonna try to rob it."

"How do they think they can do that?

"The boss got hold of some blasting powder so they are gonna blow up a section of tracks then when the train derails they will shoot the guards and take the strong box."

"Do you ever think of the families of the men you killed? What if those men guarding the train have children at home and you kill their father? Who will take care of the little children?"

"No, I try not to think too much. I let Snake do all the thinking."

"What if one of those guards was your Pa?"

"Ah my old man would never have a job like that he's too busy being drunk all the time."

"Young man do you ever think about God? Have you ever read his book, you know God wrote a book that tells us all about him and how much he loves people like you and me. Have you ever read it?"

"Naw, I never learnt no reading. I can decipher a little but I don't know how to do no readin'. Now I ain't dumb you understand I can shoot as straight as any man and I can shoe a horse and fix things."

"Would you like to learn to read? I can teach you?"

"Naw, I don't reckon I need no book learnin' I can learn all I need from Snake and the boys."

"Okay boys tamp that powder down tight under them rails and drag that fuse over this bank. When we see that train come over that rise it'll be about a mile away. I'll light the fuse and those tracks will blow up just before the train gets to this section. You gotta get it packed tight and we've gotta time it just right, it won't do no good if it goes off after the train has already passed by."

Mary Beth said, "Pa this is so exciting. We have never ridden on a train before. Just think we can be in Kansas City in just a few hours. It took all day to reach the rail line and it will only take a couple of hours for the train to travel all the way to Kansa City."

"The Lord has blessed us with a good crop and thanks to your young man and his crew we have a nice warm home. So I think it's time for your old Pa, to take you to the city and let you buy yourself some dresses that were not made by your own hands."

"I wonder if Billy Joe has ever ridden on a train. This is pretty exciting. I can't wait to get back and tell him all about it."

"And show him all your new store bought dresses."

"Pa, why is the train slowing down?"

"We are going up a small hill, soon we'll top the ridge and he'll speed up going down the other side."

Looking out the window Mary Beth, said, "It looks almost flat but when I turn my head and look back down the side of the cars I can see we are climbing. It must be a long slow grade."

"Yeah, they have to make the grades climb slowly or the engine couldn't pull all of these cars up a steep grade."

"How do they keep the train from going too fast when they have the weight of all these cars behind the engine, when it's going down the hill?"

"The steam engine and the coal tender have a chain running under them that is hooked to a heavy metal block that tightens against the wheels when the engineer pulls a long lever in the cab. The last car in the train is a brake van, it is tended by a brake man. When the engineer needs him to help slow the train, he signals with a code on the train horn. The brakeman then pulls the long brake lever in the brake van. So you have something pressing against the wheels in the front and at the back of each train. That keeps the train at a safe speed."

"Right now it looks like I could walk alongside the train."

"Yes but when he is going down the grade or on level grade he will be reaching speeds up to forty-five miles an hour."

"Pa that is amazing. Think about it, it would take two days to travel forty-five miles in our wagon."

⊨⊱ ⊰⊨

"Get ready boys, I hear him a comin'"

A rider came charging up on a lathered horse. "Snake they've got three passenger cars in this train."

"What? I was told it was only going to be freight cars and a mail car. Are you sure?"

"Snake, I was sittin' up on that ridge like you told me to, watchin' and when he came around that bend, there's three passenger cars sure nuff."

Snake started cussing and stomping around then he said, "Well it's just their bad luck. We're still gonna blow that rail. If anybody comes out of one of them passenger cars with a gun in his hand, drop him."

"Snake if that engineer don't get stopped in time that train is gonna end up down in the bottom of that gorge."

"If he's doing his job right when we blow that track he's gonna jump on the brakes. If he don't it's his fault not ours. All we want is that strong box. We get that box and we can quit grubbin' around out here for peanuts. We can live like kings. Hell I might move to Paris, France and get me one of them French women."

⊶┼ ┼⊷

The passengers on the train heard the engineer give a single toot on the train horn, then they felt the train start to gain speed. Mr. Carpenter said, "Here we go. You won't be able to walk alongside the train much longer. "

They could feel the cars starting to rock from side to side, and the clickity clack of the rail joint started getting closer together.

Mary Beth grabbed her father's arm and said, "This is both exciting and a little bit scary."

CHAPTER FORTY-SEVEN

A shiny new Pierce Arrow automobile with two well-dressed gentlemen pulled up to the saw mill. Jacob stepped out to meet them, "Good morning, what can I do for you gentlemen?"

"Are you Billy Joe McClanton?"

"No sir he's right inside the office there. Why don't you men step down and I'll take you in."

Billy Joe looked up from his ledgers as Jacob stepped in, accompanied by two men in tail coats and derby hats. "Boss these gents asked to speak to you. Fellows this is Billy Joe McClanton." He then backed out of the room.

Billy Joe stood and stuck out his hand, "Yes sir what can I do for you gentlemen today?"

One of the men said, "My name is Miles Cafton. I stopped by a few weeks ago and left my card."

Billy Joe looked back down to his desk top and said, "Yes as a matter of fact I have it right here. Have a seat gentleman. How can I be of service to you?"

For the next half hour, they outlined all of the lawlessness going on in the territory. The lawyer said, "Even though you are quite young, you have a reputation of being fast with a gun and level headed enough to know when not to use it. We have to get a sheriff appointed for the territory and we would like to get you appointed to be the sheriff."

Billy Joe looked at the two men for a few seconds as he thought over what the lawyer had just said, "I am sorry you made a trip all the way out here for nothing. You see I've got a business to run and a house to get built before I get married next spring. I can't do it."

"Mr. McClanton, we understand where you are coming from, but you need to understand everybody is busy with pressing obligations. However, if we can't find a good man to run the sheriff's department, your business and your new family will be in danger. These gangs are murdering families and we cannot get the army to send in troops to keep them in check. Roosevelt is watching the uprising in Russia, the Dutch government is in turmoil,. He is sending troops to Honduras to keep the Nicaraguan army from taking over that country. The SS Berlin just sank. The whole world is a mess right now."

"So what you're saying is, the government is too busy sending US troops all over the world, so they don't have time to protect their own citizens."

"Yes, Mr. McClanton that is exactly what I am saying. All we need is for a few good men to step up and take charge and we can make this a decent place to raise a family. I assume you are planning on having a family. I am going to, give up my law practice and allow the governor to appoint me territorial judge. Somebody has to go out and bring the bad guys in for me to pass sentence on them. I am sorry if I sound harsh, but if everybody has the same attitude that you have we will not have a safe place to raise any of our families."

"Sir, I'll admit you do make a powerful argument. Let me ponder on it a few days."

Snake yelled, "Here she comes boys get ready to blow that sucker."

"Wait a minute Snake there are passenger cars in that train."

"Their tough luck, they are just on the wrong train at the wrong time. When I wave my hat blow that sucker."

They stood watching as the engine followed by the coal tender, eased over the ridge to the east. Then ever so slowly the mail car, followed by one passenger coach, then another passenger coach, a third passenger coach and finally the break van (car used to slow the train), started picking up speed as the entire train crested the hill. At first the engineer was allowing the train to gain speed then they could hear the rumble of the steel wheels on the iron rails as she started hurtling down the grade.

Snake knew he had to time it just right, if he signaled too late the train could be safely past the break in the rails before the explosion. If he waited too long the entire train could crash down into the bottom of that gulch, but if he blew it too soon the engineer could stop and throw the train in reverse and get back over the ridge and get safely away.

It is about a mile to the ridge, I need to wait until he is a little past a half mile from the break. Right now he is about three quarters of a mile, come on engineer just a little farther. Is it getting faster?

Mary Beth looked out the window and said, "Oh Pa this thing is really going fast. Look at how fast the trees on the side of the hill are going by. This is exciting, I have never gone this fast before in my life, If it was downhill all way to Kansas City we would be there in no time."

Her father laughed and said, "Yeah, but it would sure take a long time to get back home."

Mary Beth looked at her Pa and said, "Why?"

"Because if it was downhill all the way to Kansas City it would be up-hill all the way back."

"Oh I guess that's right, maybe that is why God made small hills so it could average out both ways."

Her dad just smiled.

The train shook, and everything was thrown forward as the engineer slammed on the brakes. The sound was terrifying, the scream of metal wheels sliding on metal rails, the trail whistle bleating out a warning, a loud explosion, people screaming, the sounds mingled together, and washed over them like an avalanche.

Snake put his hands over his ears to blot out the terrible screech of metal train wheels sliding on metal rails and watched horrified as the thousands of pounds of metal train didn't seem to be slowing even with the brakes locked.

"Look out boys she's not gonna stop."

CHAPTER FORTY-EIGHT

Elizabeth had finally decided to try to make it back to the cabin. "I still don't have anything the feed the babies. Surely I can find something along the way. Maybe that cowboy who stopped by the other day will come back and bring us something."

As she cautiously neared the cabin she thought she smelled smoke, peering between the brush she couldn't see any horses around, at least she and the babies could get warm while she tried to figure something out. Carrying the baby and leading the other two she hesitantly approached the cabin. She still didn't see anybody and listening she couldn't hear any sound, slowly she pushed the front door open.

"What in the world? There is a fire in the hearth, it is down to embers but they are live coals and the room is warm. Oh, girls look we have food in the pantry. Somebody brought us some supplies."

Setting the girls down at the rough handmade table she noticed a pan half filled of warm water setting at the edge of the fire and a box of oat meal open on the shelf. "Grabbing the box she said, "Look girls we are gonna have some oatmeal for breakfast."

A few minutes later she sat three bowls full of steaming warm oatmeal and bowed her head and said, ***"God we thank you, we don't know who you sent to bring us supplies but we thank you."***

To her little girls she said, "You are mommy's big girls you can eat all of the oatmeal you want, I'll still have to help the baby."

"Did daddy bring us the supplies?"

"Honey, I don't know. Whoever it was it is sure a blessing."

Something tells me it was not my husband, I wonder if it was that cowboy, when he gave us his lunch bag he said he would be back this way? Looking around she noticed something she had not seen when she first walked in.

Mr. Yoder sat the breakfast on the table and bowed his head and said, "Lord we thank thee for the bountiful harvest that feeds us. Amen"

Slim said, "Do you really believe that there is a God up there that watches over us?"

Mr. Yoder looked up and asked, "Young man how old are you?"

"I'm twenty-three."

"The Lord has been watching over you for twenty-three years. Have you had any friends that were kicked by a horse, gored by a bull, bitten by a snake, drowned in a river crossing?"

"Well yeah, I had a friend that got bit by a snake when I was about ten years old, my saddle pard was shot by a sheriff when we tried to rob a store."

"Ever wonder why it was them instead of you?"

"I figured it was their bad luck."

"Ever wonder how an Eagle can spot a field mouse in the grass while he is flying high above? How the geese know the way back each spring after they have flown South for the winter. You see God made this world and everything in it. Let me show you something.

He reached over and picked up his Bible and opened it to Genesis page one and read, "***In the beginning God created the heavens and the earth***".

For the next two hours they read how God created the whole world and how he put people to live in the beautiful garden. Then how people sinned and God had to throw them out of the beautiful garden. Then he turned to the book of Matthew and read where God sent his only son to redeem all people who will just believe in him, when he tells them how to live.

"I always thought it was every man for himself and you had to go out and take what you wanted. That is what Snake always said."

Mr. Yoder turned back to Genesis 3:19 ***By the sweat of your face You will eat bread, Till you return to the ground, Because from it you were taken; For you are dust, And to dust you shall return.***"

"Look around you Slim, the people who are working and earning their living by the sweat of their brow, those are the people you have been hurting and taking from. They have it, you don't because they have been working and God has been rewarding them. You guys don't have anything except the clothes on your back."

"Oh but that is fixin' to change as soon as they get this job done we are all gonna be rich."

"How many other jobs have you done where you thought you were gonna be rich? What happened to each one of them?"

"Well it was just bad luck that that Ranger happened to ride up to the bank, that was when I lost my saddle pard."

Let me read to you about another man who sweated, Luke 22:44 - ***being in agony He was praying very fervently; and His sweat became like drops of blood, falling down upon the ground.***

"Jesus loved you that much Slim that he sweated blood over you and over me. Slim, Jesus loves you and he will turn your life in to a life of bliss if you will allow it, if you don't that bad luck as you call it will dog your steps every day until you end up shot down on a street or hanging from a rope. Let me read another verse for you. Joshua 24:15 - ***And if it seems evil unto you to serve the LORD,*** *choose you this day whom ye will serve; whether the gods which your fathers served that were on the other side of the flood, or the gods of the Amorites, in whose land ye dwell: but as for me and my house, we will serve the LORD.* Right now you have a choice and it is your choice, I can't do it for you and I can't make you do it one way or the other. You can continue on just as you are running with Snake and his gang or you can ride out of here go find yourself a job and start earning your way as the Lord prescribed. First, you must decide if you believe him or if you choose not to believe, because that will direct everything you do after that."

"Well it hasn't served you all that good. You let Snake and them guys beat you and cuss you and eat up all the stuff you work so hard to grow."

"God never promised we would not have hard times, he just promises to go through them with us. Who knows maybe I was put here for such a time as this so I could tell you the truth about God's love. What if a bunch of people are killed on that train to-day, but God kept you here instead of allowing you to be guilty of murdering a lot of innocent people.?"

Slim sat quietly for a few minutes with his eyes on the floor. When he looked up he said, "I don't know. Let me ask you what are you plannin' to do today?"

"Slim I am going to take the wagon out to the woods and cut some fire wood. Do you want to come help me?"

"Yes sir I believe I would."

Yoder thought, *that is the first time any of these men have offered to do anything since they came here.*

They pulled the team and wagon up next to a stand of old tress that had been damaged in the last storm. Mr. Yoder said, "Slim we'll cut the ones that have been damaged and leave the young trees."

Yoder was surprised when Slim knew how to handle an ax so well. "I see you have felled trees before."

"Yes sir, I help pa gather wood every fall. "

Even though the day was cool they were both sweating when Yoder said, "Let's take a break and eat the lunch I brought. Then we'll use the cross cut saw to cut the trunks into lengths that will fit in the fireplace and cook stove."

They sat down on the tail gate of the wagon and Yoder opened the metal syrup pail he used as a lunch bucket. Reaching in he pulled out sandwiches made of sugar cured ham and sour dough bread spread with homemade mustard." Before we eat let me ask the Lord's blessing on us.

"Dear Lord, we thank thee for this bounty that you have provided for our nourishment. Father I thank thee for young Slim here and his willingness to help me. Today father we ask thee to protect the people on the train that the other fellows are planning to rob. We even ask you to protect the robbers, may they turn to you before it is too late. Amen,"

"Mr. Yoder, no offence, but you are a strange man. Did I just hear you pray for God to bless Snake and the boys?"

"Well yes you did, you see God loves Snake and you boys as much as he loves the people on the train."

Slim just sat and looked at Mr. Yoder as he munched on the sandwich.

The two men sat on the tail gate of a wagon out where the fields met the forest and absorbed the peace and quiet. The still was only broken by the beautiful note of an occasional song bird somewhere in the trees.

After they had eaten, Mr. Yoder reached into the wagon and slid a long saw blade out of the wagon. "Slim have you used one of these before?"

"Naw, my pa didn't have one of them. In fact, we didn't have much of anything."

"Well it's real simple. See them wooden handles one on each end of the saw blade?"

"Yeah."

"You grab one end and I'll grab the other and when I push you pull, then when you push I pull and we can cut all of the big logs into short pieces pretty quick. Then we'll load them in the wagon and take them back to the house."

"They are too big around to use. I guess we'll split 'em after we get them back to the house."

"You remember that big old stump out there by the barn?"

"Yeah."

"That is my splittin' block. When we get back to the house why don't you unload the wagon and stack the wood close to the splittin' block while I go in and rustle us up some supper. Cutting wood gives a man an appetite."

"Yes sir it sure does do that, but you know what, it feels good."

Mr. Yoder just smiled and nodded his head.

CHAPTER FORTY-NINE

An army patrol heard an explosion and the screeching of steel wheels skidding on metal rails. Birds flew up in the air. A huge dust cloud billowed just over the hill in front of them. Touching spurs to their mounts the patrol raced to the crest of the hill. What they saw would haunt them for many years to come.

Sargeant McTavish shouted, "Private Sardone, ride hard to the fort and tell the doc we need him and all his supplies on the double. We have a train wreck and I see three passenger cars all mangled up. The rest of you let's get down there and see what we can do, there is people hurting down there."

Three hours later the army troops were setting up a large tent to be used as a hospital. Soldiers were shuttling in gurneys with critically injured patients into the tent. A medical corps man was evaluating each one as they came in the most critical ones were sent straight into surgery. The less critical were sent over to the medical corps men who were setting broken bones and bandaging cuts.

The dead were respectfully wrapped in a blanket and laid out in rows alongside the tent.

Mary Beth opened her eyes her mind was in a fog. Where was she? How did she get here? Who were these people milling about? Then she drifted back into oblivion.

Sometime later she was more fully awake, because she felt a lot of pain. A young army medic said, "Ma'am, it looks like you are waking up. Let me give you some water. Where are you hurting?"

Mary Beth said, "Everywhere. What happened? Where am I?"

"Ma'am. You were in a train wreck. The army has set up a field hospital, that's where you are. Let me give you some laudanum it'll help the pain." He gently lifted her head and gave her a teaspoon full of some awful tasting liquid followed by a drink of water. Soon she was back asleep.

While Mary Beth slept, the burial detail with a tired old Chaplain and a lone bugler went about the grisly task of burying the bodies of those who died in the train wreck.

The whine of the saw blade in the cool morning air was the sound that echoed through the hills. It had been going so long that birds no longer paid notice to it, they still sat high up on a limb and sang their notes

Billy Joe stepped out of the office and looked to the hills where the cutting was going on. Out of the corner of his eye movement caught his attention. Turning to his left he saw a horse coming at a fast pace. "I wonder who that can be in such a hurry?" He finished his cup of coffee and threw the dregs on the ground.

Looking closer he saw that the rider had a military uniform on. "The army must need a bunch of lumber in a hurry."

The horse and rider thundered into the lumber yard at a full gallop and the rider pulled back so hard on the reins that the horse's back legs folded under and the horse slid on its rump to a halt.

Billy Joe stepped down off the porch and said, "Whoa, soldier you're in a mighty big hurry."

"I have an urgent message for Mr. Billy Joe McClanton. Would you be him?"

"I am but why would the army be sending a fast carrier to bring me a message?"

"It ain't from the army exactly sir. It's from the army doctor."

I wonder if it's the same army doctor who took care of Lester?

The dispatch rider reached into his tunic and pulled out an envelope and handed it to Billy Joe. His hands trembled slightly as he ripped open the envelope.

It held a telegram it read:

Someone blew up the train tracks----stop--- Many dead and injured---stop—stop---- I am in army hospital---stop— no knowledge about dad----stop---come quickly--- stop --- Mary Beth.

Turning to the young soldier Billy Joe said, "Do you know where the army hospital is?"

"Yes sir, they set up a temporary hospital at the place where the train wrecked."

Billy Joe yelled for Patrick to come to him. Turning back to the soldier Billy Joe said, "Turn that horse into the corral and switch your saddle to a new one."

Patrick arrived at the edge of the porch. "What's up boss?"

Billy Joe handed him the telegram. "I'm going to grab four horses out of the corral, that way we can switch horses every so often and keep riding. You'll have to keep things going until I get back. I have no idea how long I'll be gone."

"You've got it. Do you want us to keep working on the house when we have time?"

"I'd appreciate it," with that he was off and running to the corral.

CHAPTER FIFTY

S nake and his gang jubilantly rode into Mr. Yoder's farm yard.
Looking around Snake said, "Where's that stupid kid?"

"He's not here. He no longer wants to be part of your gang."

"I guess you talked some of that mumbo-jumbo religious stuff
to him. Well to hell with him. That's one less we have to split the
loot with. "

The gang plopped four saddle bags full of money on the table
and grabbed tin cups for everyone and started filling each cup
with whiskey.

"I told you men I do not approve of whiskey in my house."

"Ha, listen to him he still thinks this is his house. Yoder, you
better get busy and get us some grub on this table or I'll show you
who is the master of this house. Now get. We've got some celebra-
tin' to do."

Then boys we got some debts to pay, not the kind you pay with
this money we got either. This money is for women and whiskey.
We're going to go back to Texas and kill that big mouth rancher
that took a whip to me, but before we do that I'm gonna kill that

whelp of his. The kid thinks he's a big shot. Got himself a saw mill and everything."

‒‒+ +‒‒

A lanky young cowboy rode up to the saw mill. Taylor saw him first and stepped out to meet him. "Howdy. What can I do for you?"

"I'm looking for a job. Y'all got any openings?"

"I'll let you talk to Patrick about that. Step down and I'll take you to see him."

"Patrick, this fellow wants to know if you are hiring."

Patrick took off his work gloves and stuck out his hand, "Howdy, my name is Patrick."

"Most folks just call me Slim."

"Well Slim it is then, come on up to the shack and let's grab a cup of coffee and talk a bit."

When they each had a tin cup full of cowboy coffee Patrick said, "I'm not the real boss. His name is Billy Joe McClanton. He had to leave on an emergency so he left me in charge till he gets back. Have you ever worked in timber before?"

"No sir, I help Pa cut fire wood every fall and cut a few fence posts so I've got a fair to middlin' idea of how to swing an ax but that's it."

"Where are you staying right now?"

"Just where ever I put my bed roll. I've just been driftin' trying to find honest work the last few days. Somebody told me about the saw mill and suggested I stop by here."

"I noticed you said 'Honest work.' You been on the hoot owl trial?"

"Well as a matter of fact I have been riding with an outlaw gang for the last few months. I was hungry and they offered me a chance to get a meal every day but they thought I was too green to let me do any of the jobs they pulled so far. They was hiding out at an Amish man's farm and when they went off to rob a train they left me behind. Me and him got to talking about God and I decided I don't want to be no outlaw so I'm looking for honest work."

"We've got a cot in the tool shed. It ain't nothing fancy but it is dry so you can bunk there until you can do better. "

"Does that mean I got a job?"

"When do you want to start?"

"Let me loosen the cinch on my saddle and I can start right now."

"Go take care of your horse and then come on back. I'll start you snaking the logs down to the sawmill. I assume you've handled a team of mules before."

"Yes sir, I handled the lines many a time."

"Slim you don't need to call me sir. I work here same as you. Come on back after you take care of your mount and I'll introduce you to the other guys."

Even though it had been cool in the early morning by mid-day the sun was beating down and it was getting hot. Jacob was running the saw blade so when the sun was at noon he pulled the cord that sent a burst of steam out through the whistle. As soon as the whistle sounded all work stopped except the two logs Slim had chained to the sled continued on down to the unloading area. Slim unhitched the two mules and led them to the corral so they could get some water and munch on hay until time to go back to work.

Slim walked over to his saddle bags and pulled some jerky out. When he got back Taylor handed him a biscuit. "Here pardner I've got an extra biscuit it'll go good with your jerky. "

"Thanks, appreciate it. I've been living on jerky and branch water for three days."

⊶⊷

Four lathered up horses and two exhausted riders stumbled into the camp where the hospital tent was set up. A sentry stepped out and said, "Halt and be recognized."

The dispatch rider said, "Corporal Swanner and a guest for people in the hospital."

"Put your mounts in the rope corral and I'll take you to the medic tent."

After they got the horses tended to, Billy Joe shook the dispatch riders hand, "Sir I sure appreciate you bringing me here. I know it was a hard ride and I thank you."

"I was glad to do it sir. I hope you find your lady is doing well. I am going to find where the soldiers sleep and take a long nap."

When Billy Joe walked into the medical tent the first thing he noticed was the medicine smell, the second thing he noticed was that they had a line of Army blankets hung down the middle of the tent. He turned and looked at the soldier escorting him.

"Sir the ladies are behind the curtain." Stepping around the make shift privacy barrier the first person the saw was an army nurse. The private snapped a salute and said, "Sargeant this here gentleman is here to see his fiancée, she was on the train."

She had a tired weary look but a gentle voice when she said, "Son what is her name?"

"Mary Beth Carpenter."

The nurse said "Thank you private. Sir if you will follow me."

When they walked up to her cot Mary Beth was sleeping. Billy Joe could see she had one leg and one arm in splints. Billy Joe looked back at the nurse who said, "You can wake her. She is just sleeping. Part of the reason is because of the laudanum I gave her so she won't feel the pain so bad."

Billy Joe touched her gently on her arm. Her eyes fluttered open then focused. A tired smile spread across her face. "Hi handsome."

"Oh honey, are you in a lot of pain? Do you feel like talking? I rode all night just to see that smile. I can come back later and we can talk. Now that I know you are alive."

By now she was fully awake, "Billy Joe don't you dare leave, just hold me. As best you can'"

Since her right arm and left leg were each in a splint Billy Joe knelt down on the dirt floor and slipped his right arm under her left shoulder. And on his knees, there in the Oklahoma dirt he gently cradled his true love to his breast.

She winced a little when his arm first slid under her shoulder then she said, "I will be better now that you are here."

"Mary Beth what happened? Where is your Pa? Is he alright?"

Tears filled her eyes. "I don't know. They won't tell me anything. Billy Joe you have got to find him for me."

CHAPTER FIFTY-ONE

Billy Joe walked into the army officers command tent. A young sergeant looked up, "What can I do for you sir?"

"Can someone tell me what happened? What caused the train to jump off the tracks?"

"Sir let me get captain Wilson. He can answer any questions you have."

The sergeant stepped through a flap into an adjoining tent. A man in a sharp creased uniform with captain's gold bars on his collar stepped smartly into the room, extending his hand he said, "I am captain Wilson, sir may I ask your name?"

Grasping the offered hand Billy Joe said, "Billy Joe McClanton, captain."

"Sir are you related to any of the victims. I don't remember seeing any one named McClanton on my list."

"My fiancée is Mary Joe Carpenter. We are supposed to be married in the spring."

"I see. Come on back into my tent and we can talk." Stepping through the flap between the two tents Billy Joe saw that they were in a make shift office with a wooden table and two wooden chairs.

Billy Joe spoke up and said, "Captain I have two questions. First, Mary Beth doesn't know anything about her father. Is he here in one of the hospital tents?"

"What is her father's name."

Billy Joe told him. The captain scanned a hand-written list, "The only Carpenter I have on my list of survivors is Mary Beth Carpenter. "

"If he is dead why hasn't someone told her?"

"Mr. McClanton, we don't have him listed on the death list either."

"Captain, how can that be, the man is ether alive or he is dead?"

"We buried thirty-two bodies on the side of the hill. Thirteen of those had no identification on them. We did save many artifacts that were in the pockets of each of those, hoping that someone could look at these items and tell us the name of the victims. There are a few survivors that are helping with the cleanup, he could be one of them."

"What is your second question?"

"What happened? What caused the train to jump off the tracks?"

"Some men set blasting powder under the tracks and blew it up as the train came down the hill. The engineer couldn't stop the heavily loaded train in time."

"Why would someone do that?"

"To get the payroll money out of the baggage car."

"Did they get it?"

"Yes."

"Does anybody know who these men were?"

"No, one outlaw called their leader a name that sounded like Snake. That is all we know."

"Did you say it sounded like snake?"

"Yes, do you know him?"

"I've met him. He and his gang came by my camp fire one evening. They are a bad lot."

"What are you going to do?"

"First with your help I am going to find out about Mary Beth's father. How much longer will Mary Beth need to be here?"

"Those broken bones are going to take a while to heal. I don't think she can travel for two months."

"Help me find out what happened to her pa. As soon as I know the answer to that I'm going to find that Snake dude and stop his reign of terror."

Walking back into Mary Beth's curtained off area Billy Joe said, "Hi sweet heart, how are you feeling?"

"The pain is not too bad they gave me some laudanum a little while ago. Did you find my pa?"

"No but I had a long talk with that young Captain. He is going to assign a couple of soldiers to help me locate your pa. Honey, I must warn you he is not listed as a patient here."

"Billy Joe I still want to know. Did you find out what happened? Why did the train crash?"

"Yes, it was a robbery. Men put blasting powder under the tracks and blew them up as the train came down the hill. The engineer, couldn't stop the loaded train in time. I am so sorry. Mary Beth the doctor said you will need to be here for six or eight more weeks for the bones to heal. I'm going to find your pa and then I'm going to find the men who did this to you."

"Billy Joe, please be careful. I couldn't stand it if something happened and I lost you too?" Tears rolled down her cheeks.

Soon after Billy Joe left the young doctor walked in. "How is my most beautiful patient doing today?"

"Thank you doctor, you are very kind but I don't feel very beautiful right now. Do you think they will find my dad?"

"Yes, my dear, we will find him somewhere, you can call me Hal, you don't have to be so formal with your doctor."

CHAPTER FIFTY-TWO

A tired unshaven Billy Joe rode into the yard at the saw mill. Taylor was the first to see him, "Well look who's back. There's coffee in the pot, grab you a cup and I'll put your horses away for you."

"Thanks, Taylor, is everything okay here?"

"Yeah, Patrick hired a new hand and he's a good 'en. It's a good thing. Because we have been cutting a lot of lumber."

A shot echoed down the canyon just as a bullet knocked chunks of wood off the door frame beside Billy Joe's head.

Billy Joe instinctively dived through the door landing on his belly. he rolled over behind the wall with his six-gun in his hand. Glancing back around the door frame he saw Taylor laying on the ground with a pool of blood spreading in the sand. Hooking the door with the toe of his boot he slammed it shut. On his hands and knees, he crawled to the gun rack and pulled down a Winchester. Crawled to the window and peered out looking for something to shoot at. He had to be careful he didn't want to shoot one of his own men.

Billy Joe saw a rifle barrel sticking out from behind a stack of sawed boards and sighted right down that barrel and squeezed off a round. The rifle suddenly cluttered to the ground as it fell over the stacked lumber. Then Billy Joe heard some rifle shots coming from up on the hill where the boys were cutting. All at once he heard horses running away from the mill. Jerking the door open he ran to Taylor. One look told him there was no help for Taylor.

Patrick came running out of the saw mill shed, "what happened, who were those hombres?"

Before he could answer, Jacob and a new man he hadn't seen before ran up. "What was that all about? We was hookin' up a sled load when we heard shootin'. I looked over and saw four or five dudes shootin' at the office, so cut loose on 'em. Oh man; Taylor got hit."

"Yes, he's dead."

"Who were those guys? Why were they shooting at the saw mill?"

"I don't know but I think we'll find one of them right over there behind that lumber pile."

The four men walked carefully over and looked behind the lumber pile. "Do any of you recognize him?"

The new man everybody called Slim said, "I know him. His name is Duke

Patrick said, "Do you think they were out to rob the saw mill?"

The new man said, "No I heard Snake brag several time about how he was going to kill a man here in Oklahoma and then ride back to Texas and kill his pa. I think they were here to kill the boss."

A grim faced Billy Joe stood looking at the dead out-law a moment then said, "What I want you boys to do is find this dude's horse and strap his body on the horse an turn it loose, it'll go back to where it's been being fed. Then I want you to build a fine box for Taylor, then we'll load it in a wagon and take him home. We'll give him a proper burial. Slim I need you to come up here to the office with me and tell me all you know about this gang."

After the casket was lowered into the ground, Billy Joe walked over to the grieving young wife and handed her two hundred dollars, "Ma'am I am so sorry. Here is a whole year's wages, this should hold you until you can decide what you want to do. If you need anything you, send word or come see me." With that he clamped his hat back on his head and stepped into the saddle.

The next day they rode into the yard of the young widow Billy Joe had helped earlier.

When they rode up Billy Joe saw the young mother timorously peek out the door. When she recognized Billy Joe she threw open the door.

Billy Joe removed his hat, "Good morning ma'am. I see you found the supplies I left you, this is Jacob, Patrick and Slim. We were riding north and I wanted to stop by and make sure you and the babies were doing alright."

"Yes, thank you. I still have the smoked meat from deer that you killed and the other supplies, so we should be okay until spring and I can plant a crop. You men want to come in I can make some coffee it won't take but a minute."

Sipping a fresh cup of coffee Billy Joe told her about the train wreck and Mary Beth being in the hospital, her father being unaccounted for. The shooting at his place.

She said, "I am so sorry. You gentlemen be careful out there.

As they started to mount up Billy Joe said, "Ma'am I never asked what is your name?"

"Sarah Thompson."

"Ms. Thompson, do you still have an ax?"

"Yes, there is one in the shed."

Billy Joe said, "Boys we are lumber men. What say we chop some more fire wood for this little lady and the babies before we ride on."

Slim who had been eyeing the young mother was the first one to grab the ax.

Late that afternoon Billy Joe and the men stopped just below the crest of a ridge on the south side of Mr. Yoder's farm. Slowly eased up until they could see over the ridge.

CHAPTER FIFTY-THREE

Mary Beth was dressed and sitting on the side of the hospital bed when the handsome young doctor came strolling in, "Well, look at my favorite patient. You are looking prettier every time I check on you. I'll tell you what your doctor prescribes for you today, I have packed a picnic basket and I have a buck-board, so I am prescribing a ride in the fresh air and sunshine to bring the color back to those beautiful cheeks. What do you say, are you ready to follow doctor's orders?"

"Doctor that is very kind of you."

"Call me Hal."

"As I was saying that is very kind of you and you are a wonderful doctor, but I am engaged to be married next spring."

"My dear you never know a lot can happen between now and next spring, but as your doctor I am telling you, you need to get out and get some fresh air and sunshine, and the best way to do that is to go for a buggy ride, even if we don't take the picnic basket. So get your coat on and I'll go get the buggy and come back for you in a few minutes." With that he turned and walked out of the tent.

━┽┾━

Looking through a pair of field glasses Billy Joe said, "I don't see any horses in the corral. I see two mules in the barn."

"That's Jake and Jon, they are Mr. Yoder's mules."

Mr. Yoder said, "I don't know where they go. They went some-where a few days ago and came back. Then a horse showed up a little later with a dead man on the saddle. The leader they call Snake he was very angry. They talked for a few minutes, told me to bury the dead man and stormed off."

"Do you have any idea where they might be going?"

"They didn't say all they said was, 'bury that piece of trash'."

Turning to Slim Billy Joe said, "Do you have any idea where they might go?"

"Probably somewhere, where there 're women and whiskey."

That night all of the guys were bedded down except Billy Joe, he was trying to think like an out-law and not being very successful about it when all of a sudden he looked up and an old Indian was sitting across the fire from him. Billy Joe jumped and grabbed for his forty-four. The old man held up his hand, "Friend, you don't need that, I have a message for you."

Billy Joe, eyed him and said, "I have met you before."

The old man just smiled, and nodded.

"What is your message?'

"You need to wake up your men and ride hard for the WF. The men you seek are on the way there with the intent to kill your fam-ily. Their goal was to kill you and then ride to Texas and kill your father. Now they are mad enough to kill the whole family. It is a hard-two-day ride from here and they are one day ahead of you."

"How do I know I can trust you? Did the out-laws send you to tell me that so I wouldn't find them?"

"Chippewa Joe never tell lie."

"Why are you doing this for me?"

"You good man. You stop bad man from killing paint horse."

Billy Joes eyes widened, "You are that Chippewa Joe?"

"Yes, now wake your men back up and get them in the saddle. You can save mother, father, and two sisters. Very bad men riding on bad mission. You stop. You can pick up fresh horses at Charlie Fetcher's place twenty miles south. I tell him you coming."

"Wait a minute old man how are you going to get there ahead of us and tell him anything?"

The old Indian smiled and then he was gone.

Startled Billy Joe jumped and splashed hot coffee on his fingers and it burned like fire. "Well I know I'm not dreaming that burns like dickens. Where did that old Indian come from and where did he go?"

Billy Joe sat there a minute more his mind in a whirl. Then he threw the rest of his coffee into the fire and started yelling to the other two to wake up,

CHAPTER FIFTY-FOUR

The sun was just coming through the slit in the tent, waking Mary Beth. The doctor walked into her area of the hospital tent. "Good morning, how is my beautiful patient today?"

"Good morning doctor. Have you found my daddy yet?"

"No sweetheart. I haven't heard a word. He sat down on the edge of her cot. "You have to face the fact; your pa may be one of those unclaimed bodies buried up on the hill. I am sorry. I know that is not what you want to hear."

"You are right, that is not what I want to hear. I will never believe that until; I see something to prove it." She started to cry.

Taking her hands in his hands and, he said, "Baby doll, don't cry I am here to take care of you."

"I know but I miss my pa."

"Where is your fiancé?"

"He has gone to track down the people who did this."

"That is so like a macho man. His place should be right here with you."

Lightening split the black sky, thunder crashed and echoed down the canyon. The rain came in blinding sheets. Viability was so bad Billy Joe and the guys had to slow their mounts to a walk.

Yelling to be heard Patrick said, "Billy Joe, maybe we should find shelter and hold up until the storm has passed?"

"I know Patrick, but we can't we've got to keep moving even if it is slow. We've got to get to the W-H and warn them. It will be bad if that bunch swoops in and attacks them without warning."

"In this blinding rain, how can you tell if we're still going in the right direction. If we get lost, we might lose more time than we will by finding shelter and stopping."

"I have been sighting on a tall peak way down south of us. Every time lightning flashes I can still see it. As long as we can still see that peak we're on the right trail."

There was suddenly a loud splash and a thump, a man screamed. Billy Joe jerked his horse to a halt. "Is everybody alrigh?."

Jacob's voice said, "My horse slipped and fell. I think my leg is busted."

"Keep talking Jacob so I can get to you. I can't see anything in the down pour. Lightening lit the sky again and Billy Joe could see Jacob on the ground and his horse struggling to regain his footing about twenty yards back up the trail. In that flash of lightening, he also saw a stand of pine trees about fifty yards to their left. Struggling through the mud to Jacob, Billy Joe opened his slicker and held it as a tent over the man and struck a match. "Hold still Jacob let me see if you are bleeding."

Patrick came into the small circle of light made by the match under his rain coat. Dropping the match Billy Joe said, "Let's get him under those pine trees, we can build a lean to."

Working quickly Billy Joe and Patrick, cut a small sapling and laid it across the branches of two trees, then chopping other small to medium size trees they started to lean them against the one suspended between the branches. Piling layer after layer of green boughs they soon had a reasonably dry lean to.

"Jacob let me get a fire going so we can have some light, then we can see how bad you're hurt."

Jacob's teeth were starting to chatter, "I 'm cold too so a fire is good."

Billy Joe and Patrick, set the bone on Jacob's leg, then split branches and formed a crude splint to hold it in place. "Handing him a cup of coffee from the pot they had placed on the fire, "here Jacob, this will help warm you and keep you from going into shock."

Slim had moved the horses up under the pine trees and tied them.

"Billy Joe we have another problem, his horse is lame."

"Oh no, let me see it." Leading the horse up closer to the fire so Billy Joe could look at the animal he said, "the horse's leg is swollen, but it doesn't appear to be broken."

All was quiet except the crackling of the fire and the pounding of the rain on their shelter. Billy Joe said, "Jacob, you obviously can't go anywhere for a while. I am not going to leave you here alone, so Patrick, let me get the supplies out of my saddle bags, you have enough to last you boys several days. This rain will probably stop came day light, then you and Slim, can rig up a travois to carry Jacob on and get him back home. I 've got to push on, those men are planning to kill my family. We know they're killers, look how many people they killed with that train wreck. "

"Billy Joe, look out there, man. You can't go on tonight. You best stay here with us until daylight. It is way too dangerous. If something like this happens to you and you are out there all by yourself you will die, then who will warn your family."

Billy Joe stared at the fire for a moment then said, "I hear what you 're saying Patrick, but I can't sit here, I 've got to warn my pa and them or die trying."

The black horse didn't want to leave the shelter of the pine trees, but Billy Joe urged him on. When lightening lit the sky again Billy Joe sighted the tallest peak again and adjusted their route slightly.

Talking to the horse Billy Joe said, "I know this is dangerous, we could walk right off a cliff or fall down into a ravine, but I am trusting that you can see better than I can, big fellow, we have got to get to the W-H before that bunch of killers do. I can't stand the thought of those mad men attacking my mother and my little sisters, Pa and Juan can take care of themselves unless they get bush-whacked. Which this bunch might very well do. My only hope is that this bunch of cowards are holed up somewhere waiting out the storm and we can get ahead of 'em."

The horse and rider started down the side of a clay hill, the big black horse slipped and almost lost his footing. The horse stopped, Billy Joe reached down and patted his rain soaked neck, "That's okay, big fellow, you are doing just fine. I know it's slick but you are doing just fine. We can do this."

With the rain pounding on his hat and running down the back of his neck he was soaking wet under the slicker. The cold was starting to seep into his bones. He thought of Mary Beth, *I hope she is still recovering. I feel bad about leaving her. She will be okay they will take good care of her until I can get back and take her home, we'll get married as soon as I got back instead of next spring, that way I can bring her home, to our new house.*

CHAPTER FIFTY-FIVE

S am had just driven into the yard. Horses shied away from the corral fence, chickens pecking in the yard, flew up on the fences, the two dogs ran under the porch. Sally Jo and the girls gathered around the shiny red Pierce Arrow automobile,

"Daddy did you buy that?"

"Yes, I did, come on and let me show you our new car."

"Sam it's really pretty. I love all the gold or brass trim."

"Wow! Mother look at these leather seats, they are pretty and feel how soft they are. They're like something you would have in a parlor."

Juan came ambling out of the barn. "Will that thing go as fast as a horse can run?"

"You Mexican bandit, it'll go a lot faster than that. This thing will go thirty-five miles in one hour.'

"Juan stay on his horse, one whole day's ride in one hour...no. You got me to ride on rail car, Juan no ride that thing. "

"Girls the top will come off if we want the sun on our faces, or we can leave it on and ride in the shade, and if it rains we have side curtains that snap onto the sides to keep us dry."

"Papa, maybe we can drive it up to see Billy Joe."

"Someday soon, that might be a good idea, for now would you three like to ride over and show it to grandpa?"

Squealing with delight the two daughters climbed in the back seat, Sally Jo slid in to the passenger seat. "Are you sure you know how to operate this thing Sam McClanton?"

"Boy, it don't get any better than this, driving a brand-new Pierce Arrow with the three prettiest gals in Texas. You girls hang on."

Looking out the side window Sally Jo commented, "That looks like storm clouds."

"Yeah, I think that storm is going to miss us, it appears to be moving north-east of us. Those people up in the Oklahoma territory are probably going to get pounded."

"I hope Billy Joe has finished his new house he wrote about. I miss that boy."

"Mother he is a man, now, he'll be getting married in the spring."

Sally Jo snuggled up against Sam and said, "I've never been happier than right now. Nothing can ruin this, I wish Billy Joe was here riding with us, that would make it perfect."

As they topped the hill they could see the Tumbling "C" spread out before them. The main house and barns looked pristine white glistening in the sun. "It looks like grandpa just had the boys put on a fresh coat of paint." Sally Jo said.

Sam looked back at the rooster tail of dust blowing up behind the back wheels. Looking at the speed-o meter on the dash board it showed he was doing twenty-three miles an hour. "It is hard to believe but this car is going twenty-three miles an hour. That means we would be all the way to Cactus Tree in less than an hour. The world is really changing girls. It really is."

One of the girls spoke up and said, "Does that mean you men won't have to wear a gun everywhere you go in the future?"

"Sweetheart, I hope so. I think we are getting there, soon law and order will be here and it won't require men to go armed everywhere they go. In fact, I started to leave my six-shooter at home for this drive."

Caroline said, "Well Pa, I feel safer when I see you have that six-shooter on. I remember that smelly old outlaw who jumped up in the buggy and tried to kiss me. Ugh!

Mattie said, "Well, pa didn't shoot him, he just took the buggy whip to him. He beat that man like a borrowed mule."

"Mattie, where did you learn that kind of talk? Sally Jo said.

Both girls giggled, "I heard Juan say it."

Sally rolled her eyes and then looked at Sam.

He kept his eyes straight ahead and tried to hide his grin.

On a hill, just north of the road sat six men on horses watching the shiny red automobile. One of them had a spy glass. That's old Sam driving that new danged contraption. I'll bet he ain't got no buggy whip in that thing."

"No but it shore looks like he's got three gals with him."

"Let's go get 'em."

"Naw, he's too close to the Tumbling C. We don't want to tangle with that bunch from the Tumbling C, that old man is a ringed tail cat with a six shooter. We'll just wait up here out of sight till they start home."

Now that it was daylight Billy Joe could see even though the rain still came down hard. He stopped at a stream that was running full and let the horse drink. Then knelt down and got a drink himself. Old buddy I know you are tired but we are almost there. As he was remounting the rain stopped. Wading across the stream the water came up to his boot tops. He was already so wet he didn't even notice. He rode on and within five miles the sun came out. Now that he could see well he recognized the area, he was only five of six miles north of the W-H main house. "Come on black horse, let's take it up to a trot, I'll see that you get a good rub down and a belly full of grain as soon as we get to the barn."

The sun was just past noon when a tired still wet rider and a tired big black gelding topped the last hill north of the ranch house for the Wild Horse ranch. Billy Joe stopped and looked for a few minutes. "Everything looks okay. I see some of the boys out there cutting hay. Looks like one of the guys is training some new horses. Nobody is shooting at them. We must 've got ahead of Snake and his bunch. Let's get down there and tell Pa what 's coming. He'll know what to do."

Riding into the yard Juan stepped out of the barn, "Senor Billy Joe. Man, where you been? You ride that horse all night?"

Motioning to the cowboy working with the horses Juan said, "Take this horse in to the barn and rub him down good then give him plenty of grain and hay."

"Juan where is Pa? I need to tell him something quick."

"Señor Sam, he not here. He bought one of them shiny new auto-mo-bels and he took the senora and the two senoritas," Juan stopped and did the sign of the cross on his chest, "God, please be with heem, he took them to ride in the auto-mo-bel to the Tumbling *C*. What is matter Billy Joe? Come into the kitchen and let's get you some hot coffee and you tell Juan what is wrong, you need to tell Señor Sam."

When Billy Joe finished telling Juan what he knew. Juan walked out in the back yard yanked out his six-shooter and fired three shots in the air as fast as he could thumb the hammer. Billy Joe saw the three men bailing hay stop and look toward the house. Juan pointed the gun back up in the air and fired three more shots as fast as he could. All three men dropped what they were doing and ran to their horses. Then Billy Joe saw two more riders appear from the ridge on the south side.

CHAPTER FIFTY-SIX

S am, Sally Jo and the girls waved goodbye to grandpa, Rosa and Russ as the Pierce Arrow sped back down the lane from the ranch house to the main road/ Sam turned the car right and headed west back to the W-H.

Caroline said, "I'll bet if grandpa wasn't so old he would like to get one of these automobiles."

"Pa, I love your new automobile, it feels so good to sit in these lovely soft leather seat and feel the wind in my hair. It is the most exciting thing we have ever done."

Mattie said, "Pa can you blow the horn?"

Sam reached over and squeezed the big red bulb attached to the end of the brass horn. AUGA-AUGA. They topped the hill and the Tumbling "C" was no longer in site.

Sam glanced over his shoulder and six masked men dashed out from the trees on the north side of the road. Instinctively he pressed the foot pedal that advanced the throttle and the car lurched forward and gained speed.

"Sam, what is the matter.?" Sally Jo said.

A bullet whizzed through the automobile between Sam and Sally Jo smashing the glass in the windshield in front of them. Then they heard the sound of more gunshots behind them.

"You three get down on the floor and hang on." Sam slammed the foot feed gas pedal all the way to the floor of the automobile. The big engine screamed and the car raced away, throwing up large clouds of dust, The road was rough, Sam was having a difficult time controlling the machine at these speeds, the rest of the glass fell from the broken windshield, Sam's hat flew off his head. The noise was incredible, the bouncing, banging, of the metal car parts, the roar of the engine straining to respond to Sam's throttle demands.

Sally Jo was on the floor as Sam had instructed but she looked up and said, "Sam who are those men?"

"Sweet heart, I don't know but they will never catch this Pierce Arrow. You girls just hang on and pray that I don't wreck it before we get to the W-H."

Billy Joe, Juan and the cowboys were standing in the ranch yard discussing what to do with the information Billy Joe had brought. Someone said, "Look at that."

All eyes followed the finger that was pointing to the ridge east of the ranch house. A bright red Pierce Arrow topped the ridge at an impossible safe speed. The only person they could see in the car was Sam. His hat was off and he was bouncing and roaring straight at them with a large cloud of dust following him.

"What is going on?'

One minute later the big red car raced into the yard and all four tires were sliding in the dirt as Sam slammed on the brakes. That is when the guys in the -yard noticed several things, the windshield was gone, there were bullet holes in the canvas top and Sam was not alone. Sally Jo, Caroline and Mattie were laying on the floor of the car.

Billy Joe said, "Pa, what happened?"

"In a minute son. Sally Jo you and the girls get into the house. Juan you and two of the guys get your rifles and get in the horse stables, Billy Joe you and the other two get up in the hay loft. I don't know who those guys are but they were shooting real bullets at my family so get ready if they come on here."

"Pa, that's why I'm here, I came to warn you they were coming."

"Billy Joe, you come into the house with me, you two guys get up in the hay loft. Grab some of those bags of feed and stack 'em across the loft door and get behind the bags. I don't know what this is all about but nobody attacks my family. We'll have 'em in a three-way cross fire, just remember where we all are don't shoot toward a barn or the house. Grab your rifles and go, they can't be that far behind me. Come on Billy Joe you can tell me what this is all about after we get inside."

As they were running to the house rifle bullets started kicking up sand near their feet. One of the tires on the Pierce Arrow exploded.

Sam yelled, "Keep your heads down boys and make every shot count."

Billy Joe jerked the window up in the kitchen and shoved his Winchester over the window ledge, six mounted men wearing masks were still about one -hundred yards out, racing toward the house, firing as they came.

Billy Joe centered the sights on his Winchester on the chest of a rider and squeezed the trigger. Everything seemed to happen in slow motion, the rifle boomed, the barrel jumped up. The rider slowly slid sideways off his horse. The riderless horse was still galloping toward the house with the stirrups flapping. Billy Joe became aware of the sound of rifles firing all around him, Sam was in the front room firing out that window, Billy Joe could see puffs of smoke coming from the hay loft and the horse stalls.

Almost as quickly as it started three masked men lay on the ground, Three mounted men could be seen fleeing toward the crest of the hill on the west.

Sam stepped out on the back porch and said, "Is everybody okay?"

Juan had a little blood on his left ear where a bullet barley nicked his ear.

"Juan, looks like you got some blood on your left ear."

Reaching up he touched his ear and it came away with a little blood on it, "Aye-chu-hua-wa, now Juan can write a new love some about the brave vaquero. Who is wounded in the fierce battle to save the ranchero."

Nervous tension caused everybody to laugh.

Looking at the three bodies on the ground Sam said, "'Do any of you know any of these dudes?"

Billy Joe said, "Yeah, these are three of the ones I came to warn you about. Unfortunately, the main one got away."

"Tell me again what this is all about."

"Do you remember an outlaw that tried to get in your buggy and kiss Caroline."

"Do you mean the little cowardly pip squeak that I took the buggy whip to?"

"Yeah, he thinks he is a bad outlaw and he swore to come down here and kill you. He tried to get me but we drove them off from my place. He lost one man there."

"Well he lost three more today. Maybe he has learned that is a bad idea."

"No, the man is crazy. I am going to hunt him down like I would a rabid coyote. I think I know where he will run to. Let me borrow your new car and I can beat him there."

"You are not going to tackle those three by yourself. "

"No, I 'll go back to the saw mill and get the three guys that work with me and we'll go dispatch these guys once and for all time."

Sam stood looking at the car for a long time like he was thinking, then he said, "Son help me put the spare tire on the car because I 'm going with you. They attacked my car while your mama and the girls were in it. I'm going."

By the time, they got the tire changed and filled the gas tank from the cans stored in the barn the sun was going down. Sam said, Bill Joe, as bad as the roads are between here and there. We may as well wait until daylight. We can still get ahead of three men on horses. They can't run those horses all the way they'll kill 'em. "

At first light two heavily armed men in a red Pierce Arrow without a windshield sped north to Oklahoma, on a mission.

Bouncing and jumping over the rough ground Billy Joe said, "This thing may be fast, but it's like riding a green bronc all the way. I've set horses that didn't buck as much as this thang."

CHAPTER FIFTY-SEVEN

Mary Beth was just waking as the sun light peeped through the slit in the tent flap when she became aware that some-one was sitting beside her cot. It was an old Indian. She gasped and pulled the cover up to her chin.

In a gentle voice the old Indian said, "Do not be afraid Mary Beth."

"You know my name?"

"Chippewa Joe know many names, you have been asking for someone to find you pa, while you are laying in the bed. Now is time for you to see what you can do to help the others who are in this hospital tent. You will find peace in helping. So, get dressed today and with the walking sticks the doctors have fashioned for you go visit the others who are hurting, and you will find in help-ing others you will find the peace you are seeking."

Mary Beth closed her eyes and thought about what the old man said, when she opened them again, he was gone. "What? Am I dreaming? Wasn't there an old Indian sitting right there a moment ago? Am I having a reaction to the medicine that have been giving me?"

She made it to the breakfast area and sat down with a cup of coffee. Doctor Hal walked in, "Oh, I see the princess is up all by herself. You must be getting stronger. Darling just don't go too fast and re-injure yourself."

"Doctor have you heard anything about my father?"

"No sweetheart, we have not. I am sorry."

"I have been sitting here thinking. I want to take my Bible and visit all of the other patients here in this tent and read some scriptures to them."

"I don't personally believe in all that mobo-jumbo but if you want to waste your time reading from a book then go ahead. I believe in science, it is modern science that has saved these from dying."

"Well, I want to do it."

"Okay, if you're going to waste your time go ahead, just wait about an hour for the nurses to complete their morning rounds. Are you ready for another picnic?"

⊷⊶

Sarah bundled the babies and took them for a walk to hunt for some more pecans. Anything to get out of that cabin for a while. The loneliness was driving her crazy. She had been so fortunate, the babies had not gotten sick, the cowboys had stocked her up with fire wood, the deer and hog they had killed and hung up would last until spring. She just wished she had someone to talk to. She talked to God, *father, I know I am supposed to be grateful for the blessing you have provided and I am, but I need someone to talk to, I need a husband to help me provide for these babies. I can't keep doing it all alone. I am sorry, I know I can depend on you but could you please bring me a good man. One who is kind and gentle, who will work hard and turn this homestead into a farm and love and provide for the girls. Amen*

As she and the girls were walking back to the cabin she stopped when she heard horses approaching. Hiding behind some brush she waited with her heart throbbing in her chest. Who can that be? I hope it is not those bad guys coming back? I don't want to hide in that cave again, it is too cold. I should have brought the gun with me. Then she recognized Billy Joe. "Oh, thank God. She stepped out and said glad to see you gentlemen. Come in I'll put some coffee on."

Pointing to a heavily armed man riding beside him Billy Joe said, "Sarah., this is my Pa. Sam McClanton. Pa this is Sarah Thompson. We stop by and make sure she and the babies are okay when we come this way. Sarah are your supplies hold ing out?"

"Yes, thank you. I know you men are cold come on in and let me make some coffee. Where are, you headed?"

Billy Joe told her about the train wreck and Mary Beth being in the hospital without mentioning the real reason they were riding hard to the north.

Sam took notice of the admiring glances between Slim and Sarah as they sipped the hot coffee she had brewed up. He also made notice of the cleanliness of the cabin and the children. *That is a good woman, she needs to find her a new husband to help her. Slim seems like a solid fellow.*

As they were getting ready to leave Slim tipped his hat and said Miss Sarah, if it's alright with you I 'll stop by and check on you and the babies when we start back this way."

She smiled and said, "that would be nice. Don't wait too long."

The sun was high in the sky when four heavily armed men stopped their horse in the edge of the woods out behind Mr. Yoder's barns.

Billy Joe said, "Slim did Mr. Yoder have any horses?"

"No all he has is two mules and a milk cow."

"Pa, I see three horses in the corral. So that must mean Snake and the other two are here."

Turning to Slim Sam asked, "What are they probably doing about right now?'

"I imagine they are in there drinking whiskey. I see Mr. Yoder out there in the field plowing so, they'll be waiting for him to stop and come in for lunch."

"Okay, here 's what I want to do. Slim you ease over there and get in the barn. When Mr. Yoder comes to put his mules up, keep him in the barn. Don't let him go into the house."

"Pa I see one of them heading for the outhouse right now. Good, Billy Joe you and Patrick slip down there and whack him over the head when he comes out then drag'im into the barn and tie him up. That 'll leave only two in the house."

Sam watched as Billy Joe and Patrick running on cat feet slipped up one on each side of the outhouse. A man stepped out buckling his belt. The man dropped like a wet flag when Billy Joe slapped up above his right ear with the barrel of his forty-four. Then Billy Joe and Patrick were running, dragging the unconscious man between them back to the hay barn.

"Good job, now tie him up good and gag him. Now we wait."

Mr. Yoder was startled when he drove Jake and Jon into the shed and found Billy Joe and two men standing there with a fourth man trussed up like a Christmas turkey laying in the straw. "What? Who are you?"

"You are Mr. Yoder. Do you know Mr. Carpenter and his daughter Mary Beth?"

"Yeah, they are my neighbors."

"My name is Billy Joe McClanton, I'm going to marry Mary Beth Carpenter come spring. This is my Pa, Sam McClanton and this is Patrick. You have some outlaws living in your house. Do you recognize that man?" Pointing to the prisoners tied up in the straw."

"Slim stepped up, "Remember me, Mr. Yoder?"

"Yes, do you remember the things we talked about?"

"Yes sir, I do and that is why we are here. We are going to take these three men back to the sheriff and turn them in. They can't go on doing what they have been doing. Do you know what they did on the trip that I was not allowed to go on?

"No, they never tell me any thing except to get busy and cook something for them to eat. They are always hungry."

"They blew up a train and killed many people."

"May the Lord have mercy on their souls."

"The Lord may have mercy on them but the law will not."

"There was six, now only three where are the others?" Mr. Yoder asked.

Sam answered, "I own the Wild Horse ranch down in Texas. These men tried to attack my family, they shot at my wife and two daughters. Three of them are dead. These three got away and we followed them here. Dead or alive we 're going to deliver them to the army who can then transport them to the nearest court house for trial if they are alive when we get there."

CHAPTER FIFTY-EIGHT

Mary Beth sat looking at the hand-written list of survivors still in the hospital tent. Doctor Hal walked up and slipped his arm around her shoulders gently pulling her to hm. "Mary Beth, you are not only beautiful, but you have a beautiful spirit. The fact that you are willing to go visit all of these patients and try to cheer them up is wonderful. I don't believe this bible mumbo-jumbo but if you do and you want to encourage the patients. Go ahead it can't hurt."

Mary Beth, pushed his arm off her shoulder, "You think you are the one healing these people. Sir, it is God who is providing the healing, you are only caring for them while God is providing the healing. Now if you will excuse me I am going to start with Mrs. Peterson and visit every person on this list and yes, I am going to pray with each one. Excuse me."

"Good morning Mrs. Peterson, my name is Mary Beth Carpenter and I was on the train when it crashed. How are you feeling this morning?"

"Honey, I'm feeling mighty poorly. I miss my John something awful. They buried him and I couldn't even get out of this bed and go see him buried." Tears rolled down the woman's face.

Mary Beth reached over and hugged her, "I know how you feel. My Pa was on the train with me and they don't even know where he is. He is not listed on this list of people alive and in the hospital tent. Nor is he on the list of those buried up on the hill. I just don't know."

Mrs. Peterson wiped her eyes and said, "Oh honey, visit all if he ain't buried up on that hill maybe he is still alive. Let's pray that you will find him and he'll be okay."

"Thank you. Let's do that but first let me read something from the Bible, what is your favorite verse?

"I like that one in John where it talks about God giving his son for us all."

"Yes that is one of my favorite too, Let me read the third chapter of John verse sixteen,

For God so loved the world, that he gave his only begotten Son, that whosoever believeth in him should not perish, but have everlasting life. (KJV)

"Oh, that is a beautiful verse," Mrs. Peterson bowed her head and said, *"Lord bless this young woman. I know you send angels among us, maybe she is an angel. Please help her find her Pa. Amen.*

Mary Beth, slowly worked her way from one hospital bed to the next. Offering prayer and kind words to all who wanted to talk. Everyone wanted to talk to the pretty young woman except the very critically injured. It had been an exhausting but fulfilling day so much sorrow and pain. Mary Beth looked at her list she only had four more names on it, her back ached, her leg throbbed, maybe she should stop for today and come back tomorrow for these last four.

She looked at the last four names: Robert Trudeau, Jerimiah Wright, Calvin Spinks, and Curtis no last name recorded.

Mary Beth squared her shoulders and with her crutch under her left arm pit she hobbled to the next bed, "Good afternoon, Mr. Trudeau,"

An older man opened his eyes, "Are you a nurse?"

"No sir, I am a patient like you. I was on the train. "

"Why 're you here?"

"I am better, with this crutch I can move around, so I decided rather than sit there feeling sorry for myself, I was going to visit all, of my fellow wounded travelers. Would you like for me to read a bible verse for you or pray with you, or just itt and talk? What can I do for you today?"

"You can go away I don't need nobody to do nothing for me." He turned over and faced the wall.

Mary Beth opened her Bible to Numbers chapter six and looked down to verse twenty-four and read:

Numbers 6:24-25, King James Version (KJV) The Lord bless thee, and keep thee: The Lord make his face shine upon thee, and be gracious unto thee: ..

As Mary Beth limped to the next bed she prayed, "Lord I didn't need that man's attitude this late in the day. I am tired and weary, give me the strength to carry on for three more beds."

The next one was asleep and she didn't want to wake him so Mary Beth simply stopped and said a prayer for the person and looked at the note reminding herself that this person simply had a first name listed. The only name listed on the paper was Curtis.

—⊷ ⊶—

Mowatt, stroked his tobacco stained beard. I need me a woman. I think I'm gonna go back over there to that cabin and see where that little filly got off to. I know that dude had a wife and a couple of young'uns. She could have gone anywhere."

"Well there sure wasn't no woman there the day we went over there."

"I know that you lunk head, but he had a wife so where is she? I need that woman, by harry I'm gonna go get her. After all she's a widow now so she needs a man to take care of her needs. That's me."

"You gonna just ride over there and grab her and throw her over your shoulder like a sack of feed and bring her back?"

"Well if she don't want to come on her on, I might do that. "

"What are you going to do with the youngens?"

"I don't know. I don't need no youngens hanging around getting snot all over ever thing."

"Well Mowatt, if you get the gal I guess you'll get her land too. That way you have over twelve hundred acres. You'll have the land on both sides of the creek. Now you know this ain't no dance hall gal, you got to treat her lady like until you get here back to your house."

"Yeah, I guess you're right but I got a powerful need right now."

"You know and I know you can get yourself hung out here in the west if you don't treat a lady right. Now after you get her moved in the house with ya, that's a different thing."

"So, what're you suggestin'?"

"I say we wait until in the morning, then you get all cleaned up and hitch up the buck board and ride over there real neighbor like and talk to her. Tell her you got this big cattle ranch and you want to take her and them youngens home with ya and take care of 'em. That way she can holler all she wants to if she don't like the way you treat her but ain't nobody gonna listen cause she moved in on her on free will."

"Alright pass me that jug of whisky. I'll wait till morning then I'm gonna go get me a woman."

CHAPTER FIFTY-NINE

S am stepped out of the hay barn and yelled, "Snake, we've got
Mr. Yoder and your man Tucker out here in the barn. Throw out
your guns then come out with your hands where we can see 'em."

There was no sound from in the house. Sam raised his voice
and said, "Snake this is Sam McClanton from the Wild Horse
ranch. You shot at my automobile with my wife and daughters in
it. I come to get you and I ain't leaving without you. Now you can
come peaceable and go take your chances with a judge or me and
you can settle this right now. You are gonna come out of that house
if I have to burn it down to get you out. You are gonna come out."

"Did you come all the way from Texas up here?"

"Yep I sure did. You should a knowed better than to shoot at my
family. I would have trailed you all the way to Canada. Now what's
it gonna be, you gonna come out and face me or face the judge?"

"If I throw down my gun how do I know you won't shoot me
down as soon as I walk out the door?:"

"You have my word for it. If you two throw out them guns, we'll
load you in a wagon and haul you to the court house. Better make

up your mind pretty quick my patience is getting kind-a thin I 'm about ready to set that place on fire. "

"Pa, you're not really gonna burn down Mr. Yoder's house are ya?"

Sam looked at Mr. Yoder and said, "No sir, I ain't gonna burn down your house but Snake don't know that."

"Snake what's it gonna be?"

A shot rang out and a bullet hit the side of the barn. "McClanton, I think you are bluffing. A good church going man like yourself will never burn down Mr. Yoder's house to get me out. There's enough food and water in here to last till spring. It's warm in here I think I'll just stay."

"Billy Joe, you see how the cabin doesn't have any windows on the east end? You and Slim ride around and approach the cabin from that end," Sam said.

"Snake you are down to two minutes. I will set that cabin on fire if you don't come out. Now you have two choices you can keep your gun on and face me like a man or you can throw out your gun and face the judge but I will burn you out. What's it gonna be?"

"McClanton, you're bluffin', Yoder is with you, you ain't gonna burn his house down."

"Snake, you 've got to be a stupid man. My son owns a saw mill, I can build Mr. Yoder a new house any time I want. At least save your man. Tell him to come on out with his hands up and we'll put him in the barn with your other man."

"He's got good drinkin' whiskey in here. You ain't got any out there do ya?"

Sam was watching Billy Joe and Slim approach the cabin from the blind side. He could see what they were doing and he knew that Snake could not. "one last time Snake. You and or your man come on out or I will fire that cabin."

A rifle bellowed and a bullet smacked into the side of the barn.

Sam watched as Billy Joe rode up beside the wall on the east end where the fire place chimney was. Slim dismounted and grabbed

Billy Joe's horse bridle so the animal would stand still. Then Billy Joe stood up in his saddle and draped one of the canvas wagon sheets over the top of the chimney. Then he dropped back down in the saddle, Slim released the hold on Billy Joe's horse, jumped back on his own horse and they both rode away. Circling back to the hay barn.

All at once they could hear coughing and gagging going on in the cabin and the back door flew open. A rifle and pistol flew out and landed in the dirt. Snake's man ran out through the smoke with his hands up.

Sam called to him and said, "Keep coming to my voice with them hands up you've got three guns trained on you right now. "

"McClanton, if I come out without my guns on, are you going to shoot me down as soon as I step through that door?"

Billy Joe said, "Don't do it Pa. don't give that scum bag any chance. "

"You walk on out in the yard Snake, and I'll give you a minute to clear the smoke out of your eyes, You'll get your chance. "

"Let me take'em Pa."

"Not this time son, this is personal, he tried to kill your ma and your sisters."

Snake appeared out of the smoke, he was coughing and gagging. Sam never moved he simply stood glaring at him. When Snake finally got his breath back and wiped his eyes with his handkerchief, Sam McClanton was standing not ten yards in front of him.

Snake snarled, "You are the mangy dog that whipped me with a buggy whip. I have been living for the day I could kill you. Look at my face your whelp did that. After I kill you I'm going to kill him too."

"You can't do it talking about it." Sam quietly said.

Snake snarled like a dog and as fast as lightning his hand whipped down for his six-shooter. Something was wrong. His gun was not rising, his knees were buckling, something slammed into his chest. Nobody could beat him. His eyes rolled back and then all was dark.

Sam slowly fed two new shells into his forty-four. "Pa are you alright."

"Slim ride around there and get that tarp off Mr. Yoder's chimney so he can air out his cabin. Then let's get these three loaded up in the wagon and haul all three to the federal court house. Then Billy Joe you go check on your fiancée, I am going to check on Sally Jo and the girls."

Slim said, "Sir if it's alright with you I 'm going to ride back down and check on Sarah and the babies. "

"You do that Slim, that Sarah is a good woman, and she needs a good man. You take care of her and the babies. If you ever need anything, come see me." Sam said.

CHAPTER SIXTY

M ary Beth hobbled wearily to the last hospital bed. She was tired, and sad, so much pain and misery, some with very little hope. She really didn't want to see another broken body to-day. She stopped and prayed, *Father, give me the strength to minister to this last poor man. We don't even know his last name, but father you know even the sparrow that flies, so I know you know this poor man. Please give me the strength and the words you want him to hear. Amen*

Making her way to the side of the bed Mary Beth, could see this shrunken skeleton of a man, his head swaddled in fresh bandages covering the top of his head down past his ears, his cheeks covered with grey beard, he looked old and weak. His eyes were closed, she paused to make sure he was breathing.

She opened her Bible to the twenty-third psalm and started reading: The Lord is my shepherd; I shall not want.

2 He maketh me to lie down in green pastures: he leadeth me beside the still waters.

3 He restoreth my soul: he leadeth me in the paths of righteousness for his name's sake.

4 Yea, though I walk through the valley of the shadow of death, I will fear no evil: for thou art with me; thy rod and thy staff they comfort me.

The man's eyes fluttered open and a weak voice said, "Is that you Beth."

Mary Beth was so startled she dropped her Bible, and screamed, "Pa,, is that you, Pa?"

The nurse hearing her scream came running, "What 's wrong?"

Mary Beth couldn't answer, she was sobbing and hugging the man in the bed, she said, "His name is not Curtis, this is my Pa."

⚜

Slim rode into the yard and called, "hello the house."

The door cracked open and someone peeked out. Then it flew open and Sarah stood in the open-door way, "Oh, you did come back. Come in."

As Slim stepped down another horse rode into the yard and stopped in a cloud of dust. A swarthy old man with a pot belly and chewing tobacco all in his beard demanded, "What are you doing here, this is my woman, get back on that horse and get out of here?"

Slim looked at Sarah. She said, "I don't know this old man."

"Honey you 're going to, I come to take you and them youn-guns home with me and I'm gonna take good care of ya."

"Mister, I don't know you, all though I saw you one time before when you and some more men tore up my cabin. I am not going to go anywhere with you."

"Mister you heard the lady. You best get back on that horse and ride out of here right now."

"By thunder I'll show you, you young whipper-snapper." He reached for his six-gun.

Before the gun cleared the leather holster, Slim stepped forward and his right fist impacted the point of the man's chin. The man's head snapped back like it was on hinges and his boots flew up off the ground. He landed flat on his back in the dust.

Bellowing lie a raging bull he came off the ground surprisingly fast for an old man. He reached for his gun again, but it had fallen out of the holster when Slim hit him. The old man lowered his head and charged, swinging both fists as fast as he could.

Slim ducked under the wildly swinging fists and slammed two hard blows to the man's belly. Slim heard the air whoosh out of the man's lungs. But the old boy was a fighter. A huge right fist caught Slim on the left side of his head and spun him around, stars flashed in Slim's head.

Sensing he had the advantage Mowatt waded in with both fists. Slim grabbed him and threw him over his hip, the old man landed with a thud on the ground. This time he was a little slower getting up. Slim waited until he was on his feet then waded in with a left hook that split the old man's ear, followed by a right cross that almost lifted him out of his boots. Mowatt hit the ground and stayed there.

Slim was startled when he realized there was a man sitting on a horse at the edge of the clearing. "I say laddie. You are quite deft with those mitts. Ya, need a little more practice, ya shuda had him several minutes ago but ya, did alright."

Slim was getting his breath back, he looked at Sarah. "Do you know this man?"

She shook her head no.

"Aye allow me to introduce me-self, laddie, I am reverend McCelvey, I am traveling through and saw the chimney smoke and thought there might be someone here who needed a man of the cloth. Wasn't expecting so lively a welcome."

It was then Slim noticed his collar. "Where are you from reverend?"

"I am from the County Cork, by way of Boston and I am taking the Lords word to all in this untamed land. Can I be of service to you and the misses?"

Slim looked at Sarah and said, "Yes sir, please come on in, I'm sure Sarah will have some coffee, and we can talk about how you can be of service to us, that is if she is willing."

Sarah smiled and said, "Coffee will be ready in just a minute."

Mowatt was waking up, when the reverend said "Laddie, shouldn't we help the man back on his horse so he can continue where he needs to be going."

"Yes sir, first let me take his guns, then I'll tie his hands to the saddle horn and send the horse home."

Sam clasped Billy Joe on the shoulder and said, "Son, you go get that pretty little fiancé of yours and bring her down to the W-H so ma and your sisters can get to know her. You know your ma, we'll have the gal-dangedest wedding in the country for you two."

"As soon as she and her pa, can travel we'll be down. First, I'm gonna order me one of those automobiles. I saw how fast that one got us up here."

Two days later Billy Joe rode up to the hospital tent and the first thing he saw was Mary Beth and her father sitting on a bench soaking in the sun.

She saw him and jumped up, "Billy Joe!" Running to him.

Billy Joe reached down and scooped her up in his arms., kissing her as he pulled her to his breast.

"Oh darling, I have been so worried, I imagined all kind of bad things happening. Did you find that awful man? Is he in jail where he belongs?"

"He is not in jail,"

"Oh, does that mean he can still come back and hurt us?"

"No unless he has a key to get out of hell."

"What? Is he dead?"

"Yes, darling he is very dead. Is that your pa sitting there?"

"Oh yes, isn't it grand? He was here all along, they just didn't know his real name until he came to. Let me down and come talk to him."

Billy Joe gently let her down then stepped down off the horse and walked over to the bench. "Good morning sir, how are you?"

"I'm getting stronger every day. How is your new house coming along?"

"That is what I wanted to talk to both of you about. It is finished." Turning to Mary Beth he said, "Honey the boys have done a great job, the house is finished, would you consider moving the wedding up so I can take you and your father home to our new house?"

Mary Beth threw her arms around his and kissed him, "Yes."

"Mr. Carpenter, how soon can you two travel?"

"I think the doctor is about ready to let me go home. The problem is I don't think I can sit a horse for three days."

Mary Beth said, "We could get a buggy,"

"Wait a minute, my dad had an automobile and we made it all the way up here from Texas in one day. I want to get one of those thigs anyway. So I'll ride over to Oklahoma City and buy one. When I get back we can make it home in about five hours. You talk to the doctor and I'll go get us an automobile."

"Son are you sure those things are safe?"

"They're safer than the train was."

Two days later Billy Joe loaded Mary Beth and her father in his brand new shiny black Model T Ford.

"Billy Joe, are you sure you know how to drive this thing?"

"Yes ma'am, I done drove it all the way from Oklahoma City to here."

Mr. Carpenter said, "Since you eliminated Snakes bunch, is everything quiet now?"

"No sir, not exactly. It seems to be pretty quiet down in my area but I have been hearing of some bloody goings on up here in the north part. Some folks think Bloody Bill Henderson and his bunch robbed and killed a family over by Bartlesville a couple of weeks back and a bunch called 'the wild ones' have been robbing and killing over around Jefferson."

"I thought those two were up in Kansas and Missouri."

"They have been but I guess its getting too hot for them so they may have moved down here."

"What I hear those two gangs are guerillas left over from the war, and they don't just rob. They kill their victims every time."

"Sir, they are really bad. They don't kill the women right away. If you get what I mean."

"Billy Joe, I know exactly what you mean and that is disgusting. Robbing is bad, killing is worse, but to do that to a decent woman, is madness. Those cutthroats need to be hunted down and destroyed just like you would a rabid wolf."

"Sir I agree, the only way those animals would ever lay a hand on Mary Beth, they would have-ta kill me first."

Mr. Carpenter was quiet a moment then said, "Which is what they usually do."

"Sir?"

"They usually do, the cowardly scum usually do kill the men first."

"All the more reason we are going to get in that shiny new Ford automobile right after breakfast in the morning and we're getting out of this part of the state."

CHAPTER SIXTY-ONE

The next morning right after breakfast, they loaded up in the new Ford automobile.

"Mr. Carpenter are you comfortable back there?"

"Yes, the seats are soft and this lap robe makes it real cozy."

Billy Joe reached in and adjusted the throttle then walked around in front of the vehicle and grabbed the steel crank attached to the front of the motor and gave it a hard turn. Nothing happened. He walked back and readjusted the throttle and walked back to the front of the vehicle. This time he gave a hard turn on the crank and the engine roared to life. Walking back to the driver's side door he climbed in.

"It looks like we may get into some rain but at least in this automobile we won't get rained on. If my navigator up here can help me find the road home we should be there in time for a late lunch. If either one of you is uncomfortable or need to stop for any reason just sing out."

As Billy Joe herded the bouncing rattling vehicle over the roads made for horses and wagons. The rain came pouring down. "Mary Beth, I'm glad we are in this Ford, instead of on a horse."

"Yes, we're at least not getting wet, but a horse is easier to ride, It doesn't bounce as much." She said laughing.

Billy Joe reached over and made a big show of patting the dash of the automobile, "Don't be offended little Ford, she was only joking. You are doing just fine." The front wheel hit a rut in the road and the vehicle lurched sideways almost turning over on its side.

Grabbing the steering wheel with both hands Billy Joe managed to get the vehicle straightened out.

"Billy Joe, maybe you need to slow down. Are you okay?"

"Honey, I'm fine."

Things settled down, the road appeared to get a little smoother, the rain kept coming down hard, the wind rocked the car from side to side often.

"Mary Beth, do you want to stop in the next town we come to and see if we can find a preacher and get married today or do you want to wait until we get there and have a chance to plan a proper wedding?"

"I would love to have a big wedding. We can't both live in the house until we get married and we don't have two houses so maybe we should stop and find a judge or a preacher."

"Honey that is not a problem, I have been living in the back of the mill office for over a year. I will simply stay there until we can plan a real wedding. We can invite mom and dad and the girls, They would love to come to a wedding. What do you think Mr. Carpenter?"

"I think you two are doing just fine, you don't need any input from me. Either way s fine with me. I think I'll curl up in the throw and take a nap."

The road suddenly dipped down into what appeared to be a raging river, Billy Joe stopped the vehicle and said, "I need to get out and look at that it may be too deep to cross."

Billy Joe reached up and pulled his hat down tight on his head and stepped out, in a moment he was back, soaking wet. "That creek is running fast but doesn't appear to e too deep. "

"Billy Joe, do we dare chance it?"

"This rain could go on for hours, so unless we want to stay here for several hours we have to chance it because there's no other way to go. "

Looking at Mary Beth, *if we stay here we don't have any food, it's going to get cold after dark. Mr. Carpenter doesn't need to stay out in a cold car overnight. However, if that water is deeper than it looked we will be washed away in the flood. We will all probably drown. At least they will find our bodies in the car when someone finds it someday.* Looking at Mary Beth, *I sure don't want to lose her like I Might in a flood,* looking over his right shoulder at Mr. Carpenter huddled up in the lap robe. *We can't sit hear and let him get chilled when the temperature drops, it's cold enough already.*

After a few more minutes of hesitation he said, "Mary Beth find something you can hold on to because it may get real rough." Turning to the back seat he said, "Mr. Carpenter, you need to wake up sir, because I am going to have to ford a flooding stream and it could get real rough."

Billy Joe gripped the steering wheel and looked through the rain streaked windshield and blinked his eyes and looked again, there stood a soaking wet old Indian pointing to the right side of the road, he seemed to be saying drive over on that side.

CHAPTER SIXTY-TWO

Six weeks later.

The church was filled with flowers and bunting. In the yard was Billy Joe's Ford that Patrick and Slim had decorated from top to bottom with just married signs, ribbons and some empty bean cans. Three or four automobiles all from Texas, and an assortment of wagons, buggy's, buckboards and saddle horses. Everybody that had ever bought lumber from Billy Joe's saw mill was there.

As soon as the wedding was over the preacher announced, "You are all invited to stay so we can show these folks visiting from Texas that we know how to throw an old fashion Oklahoma Bar-B-Q. Out behind the church some of the boys have a half a steer on a spit and they have been roasting it all night. Now the bride and groom are gonna get in that Ford automobile and go off and do whatever brides and grooms do but the rest of us are gonna have us a Bar -B-Q." He smiled as he said, "Rumor has it that there might be a jug or two back there, it's a good thing I'm a Methodist instead of a Baptist."

www.ingramcontent.com/pod-product-compliance
Lightning Source LLC
Chambersburg PA
CBHW051644260626
47170CB00004B/1320